CHRISTMAS IN THE AIR

JOSIE RIVIERA

This book is dedicated to all my wonderful readers who have supported me every inch of the way.

THANK YOU!

PROLOGUE

*P*enelope Reid sat glued to her seat.

Breathe in. There's nothing to be nervous about. Flying in an airplane is routine for many businesspeople.

And she, unfortunately, was a businessperson.

She attempted to smile at the flight attendant who walked past, before resuming her pep talk to herself.

Virginia to Hilton Head Island is a short flight.

She considered texting her brother, Lincoln, with a 'mission accomplished' message, though he wouldn't get the message until she had cell service again. He'd encouraged her to take the flight to secure a toy shop location. She'd complied, albeit reluctantly, though she'd been successful with the negotiations and closed on the deal. Nonetheless, when she finally arrived home, she intended to wring his neck. He knew how much she dreaded flying.

She cut a glance at her handsome seatmate's profile. She'd admired the angle of his face—his sharp jawline and straight nose—throughout most of the flight. Framed by the afternoon sunlight streaming in the window, he seemed relaxed.

1

Of course, he seemed relaxed because he was sleeping. In fact, he'd slept almost non-stop.

She coughed and nudged him with her elbow. She needed someone to talk to and take her mind off the flight. She'd already breezed through every magazine in the seat pocket.

"Hmm?" He took off his aviator sunglasses and turned toward her. His eyes were a deep shade of brown, warm and mesmerizing, rimmed with black eyelashes. His skin exuded a healthy golden glow. "Have we arrived?"

"Hardly."

He peered out the window. "Cloudy day."

"The weather forecaster called for rain."

"He was probably right."

"*She* was probably right," Penelope corrected.

He grinned. "Touché."

Penelope sat up straighter. "Before you fell asleep, we were discussing our jobs."

"Were we?"

"We were about to." Her seatbelt tightened as she leaned toward him. "I've managed a toy shop business ever since I was a teenager."

"Sounds fun."

"I hate it."

His dark eyebrows curved upward. "Why?"

"Do you want the truth?"

"By all means."

"I shouldn't be telling you this, but I've never been good at deception."

"Bravo." He gave her a thumbs-up. "So, do tell."

"I'd like to do something else."

"Nothing wrong with that. I'll keep your secret." He flashed her a positively magnetic smile.

Her heart stilled. Here sat a good-looking man who had listened to her rattle on about her life whenever he opened

2

his eyes. At least, she assumed he listened. She'd held him captive because he couldn't escape. They were seated next to each other in first class. Still, she'd begun to assume they were friends, and he was an attentive guy.

At his assessing gaze, a flush warmed her cheeks. "I'm bored with my job. I want to create, not manage."

"Create what?"

"I'm not cut out for left-brained, logical analysis anymore. Let's call it a midlife crisis."

"Let's." Another smile. "Do you have another job lined up?"

"No."

"Is your job difficult?" His tone lowered. Thick, wavy hair fell across his forehead, and he pushed back the strands with his hand. His features were a bit weathered, his jawline and cheekbones prominent. A rugged man who apparently spent time outdoors if appearances were any indication.

The thump of attraction in her chest surprised her. She hadn't felt an interest in any guy since her divorce.

"No, my job isn't difficult," she said. "Just repetitive."

"Playing with toys can't be all bad."

She stiffened at his off-hand remark. If he was teasing, he wasn't funny.

"I don't play with toys and they're not mine," she clarified. "I *manage* the business and we sell toys."

He cocked an eyebrow. "We?"

"My brother and I."

"No husband?" He sounded as if he accused her of something—she wasn't sure what—because of her marital status.

"No husband."

"So, you're in the family firm. Come on, mate. Toys are heaps of fun."

Mate? Inwardly, she shook her head.

"Bloody tough, then?"

Bloody? Who used these terms?

"I've done the same job forever." She gave herself a second to regroup. "Since I was a teen."

"When you decide what you want in life, focus on it and let go of the old ways," he replied. "Embrace your creativity."

"At my age?"

"At any age."

He scratched a finger along the shadowy bristles on his jaw. Wasn't it time he shaved? Come to think of it, he looked as if he hadn't slept soundly in a week. His jeans were clean, though his green cotton shirt was rumpled.

He paused to consider her—regarding her cream-colored crepe blouse, which she'd managed to spill coffee on that morning—and her stretchy brown slacks. She hadn't had an extra minute to put on an ounce of makeup before rushing through the Richmond, Virginia, airport to catch the plane to Hilton Head Island. In her hotel room, she'd only showered and added a light spritz of her favorite lavender-scented perfume.

She hardly traveled anywhere anymore, and a commute to Virginia was a last-minute meeting she couldn't avoid. She didn't even like going to Virginia, because it reminded her of her old life and her ex.

To make matters worse, she'd overslept. The evening before, she'd overindulged in fried food and two glasses of celebratory wine.

Conversation was easy when her seatmate didn't stare at her. But now that he was wide awake, she was unprepared for his assessing gaze.

She brushed nonexistent lint from her slacks. "What should I do for a living? Any suggestions?"

Mr. Too Handsome for his own good, she added to herself.

"There are heaps of books on the subject. Whatever suits

your skill level and interests." He gave a short nod, turned back toward the window, and slipped on his sunglasses.

"I'm excellent at parenting, although my son disagrees," she said. "I'm a single mother of a soon-to-be teenager and life isn't easy."

"No matter the age of the child, parenting calls for patience."

"Do you speak from experience?" she asked.

"Nope."

"Do you have kids?"

"Nope. Never will."

Why? she wondered. She grabbed a candy bar from her purse and took a nibble, debating on whether to ask him to explain. However, he kept his face turned toward the window. In under two minutes, she detected soft breathing. Most likely, he was asleep again.

"I'm divorced and my ex has remarried," she said. "His twenty-something wife was a coworker, and she is decades younger than me." Penelope added another fact that continually gnawed at her. "They're blissfully happy and expecting a baby."

"Are congratulations in order?" her seatmate mumbled.

"Not on my end." She tried to push down her snide comment and found she couldn't. "I find it all a bit odd, considering my ex's age." Resentment boiled inside her when she least expected. "He'll be in his seventies by the time their child graduates from college."

"What's your ex's name?"

"Roy."

"Mmm."

She stopped speaking for a second to gain control of her voice. "He moved to another state, making our shared custody agreement for our son trickier than ever."

Her seatmate nodded slightly.

"You know what else?"

He still faced the window. "Hmm?"

She bit off a piece of candy, chewed, and swallowed. "All the guys I've seen since my divorce are cads. I subscribed to an online dating website, but my first date proved an embarrassing bust." She didn't elaborate, and he didn't ask. She'd also dated an art teacher at her son's school until the man gave up. He was a pleasant guy, but her feelings for him had been absent. Plus, he'd acted as if her son didn't exist.

She'd resolved herself to the fact that she wouldn't commit to anyone ever again. Her heart couldn't recover from another broken relationship. Living inside the cocoon of a quiet, safe environment was preferable and assured no one got hurt.

"In summary," she finished, "I've decided to stop dating altogether."

"An archaic term," he replied.

"Dating?"

"Cad."

She waved a dismissive hand. "I refuse to be forced into any more awkward conversations at the local pizza joint."

"You don't like pizza?"

"I like all food."

"Then never say never."

"What's that supposed to—"

The plane jerked. Several shrieks from passengers rang throughout the plane.

Penelope joined in the shrieking, louder than the rest. Her half-eaten candy bar dropped to the floor.

Her seatmate swiveled to her and pocketed his sunglasses. "Are you all right?" His gaze darted about the plane's cabin before landing on her.

"Didn't you feel the plane?" she asked.

"It's just a bump."

"I'm afraid of heights."

"You're on a plane," he reminded.

"I had no choice. I was forced to close on a business deal." She hadn't had a spare moment for anxiety to grab hold when her brother had booked the last-minute flight, and hindsight did little good. She'd assured herself there was nothing to fear.

Envision floating above pearly fluffy clouds while drinking a glass of sparkling water, she told herself.

What was it about reality that proved so different from your imaginings?

She indicated the window—they were flying above *gray* clouds, not pearly, and they weren't at all fluffy.

"To keep my mind off of the fact we're thirty-five thousand feet in the air, I've babbled constantly," she said.

"You talked. You haven't babbled. Talk all you want." He reached into his pocket and handed her a clean white handkerchief. Despite the plane's cold temperature, she was sweating. He'd noticed the sweat beads on her forehead before she had.

"You haven't told me anything about yourself," she prompted.

"What would you like to know?"

She glanced at his left hand. No ring. He wasn't married, although the lack of a wedding ring didn't mean anything.

Regardless, she asked, "Are you married?"

"Absolutely not. Once was enough."

"You're divorced?"

"Thankfully divorced. Marriage isn't for me."

"Why not?"

He shrugged. "My career is important and all-consuming. Romance, women, and marriage got in the way."

She took several seconds to digest his information.

Got in the way of what? she wanted to ask.

7

"Planes are remarkable if you stop to analyze the mechanics," he said.

"Now is not the time to analyze how planes stay in the air." She dabbed at her forehead with his handkerchief. Her hands were clammy. "Never again," she muttered.

"You won't ever fly again?"

She twisted her wristwatch. "I'll drive or take a bus or a train."

"Have you always been afraid of flying?"

"No. Only the past few years."

"Suppose you're traveling overseas?" he asked.

"Are you kidding? I'll never fly overseas."

When the plane bounced from side to side, she grabbed hold of his arm. Her throat went dry. A fresh start of panic stunned her as the fasten seat belts sign flashed.

Flight attendants buzzed through the cabin, reminding the passengers to buckle up, before scurrying to their own seats. The captain came on the intercom and assured that the plane was flying outside of a thunderstorm, and the occurrence was brief and passing.

Penelope tugged at her seatbelt, ensuring she was secure. Her seatmate patted her shoulder, making no attempt to move away or disentangle his arm from her death grip.

He was tuned in to her fear.

Maybe he was attracted to her—despite the deepening lines around her mouth and the dark circles under her eyes. She didn't need to peer at herself in a mirror to realize she looked a sight. She never seemed to get a sound night's sleep anymore and blamed her restless, worried thoughts on her son for keeping her awake at two a.m.

She dropped her hand and passed him his handkerchief. "Is Hilton Head Island your final destination?"

"No. You?"

"I'm staying overnight on my brother's houseboat, then

driving on to Roses in North Carolina," she said. "You may have heard of the town."

Roses combined small-town charm with big-city conveniences. The tidy homes blended with the landscape of the scenic mountains. In the summer, the town was renowned for bubbling hot springs and comfortable mountain temperatures.

A look she couldn't read flickered across his tanned face. "You're staying on a houseboat?"

"Southern summers are intense, and the ocean breeze is a welcome respite, especially at night."

"Houseboat living is ... different; I'll grant you that. As for me, I'll stay on land, thank you very much."

"Or in the air," she reminded.

He laughed out loud. "You live in Roses?'

She nodded. "Roses is my childhood home. I moved away after college and got married, then returned after my divorce. Since then, I haven't made many friends."

At first, familiarity had enfolded her like a generous hug. Now, things had changed.

"Why not?" he asked.

"Friendships are difficult. The women at my son's school have a close circle reaching back to when their kids were in kindergarten. I missed all that." She cast a glance at him. His expression was unreadable. "Don't get me wrong. Roses is lovely. The main street is lined with local shops, and the park boasts a bandstand for outdoor concerts."

"I prefer big cities. I like all the restaurant options and public transportation."

"Roses is unique and has loads of restaurants."

"I'm sure the town is a beaut." His gaze lingered on her face. "Care for a cold one?"

"I don't drink," she said. "Correction. I don't drink often."

"I used to say that."

"And *now* you drink?"

"Depends on the circumstances."

"The flight attendants are buckled in." She indicated them with her chin.

"They'll be up and about soon."

"You fly a lot?"

"Sometimes," he said. "I've experienced turbulence, though flying is safer than any other form of transportation."

"A quote from …?"

"Me." He smiled. "In all fairness, I read the statistic in *Popular Science* magazine."

"Are you trying to reassure me with a magazine quote?"

"I'm a pro. My job is all about counseling and prevention."

He opted for a caffeinated soda when the flight attendants came to their feet and began serving passengers one last time. He picked up Penelope's candy bar, murmuring, "Your sweet fell on the floor," and handed the candy to the attendant to discard.

"No cold one?" she asked him.

He raised his glass. "I'm a fan of America's free refills."

She'd noted his accent. Probably Australian.

Penelope ordered a low-calorie lemon-lime sparkling water.

"I prefer coffee," she informed him. "In fact, I'm obsessed, and drink six cups a day."

"You didn't order coffee."

"I take my coffee with loads of cream and sugar. Low-calorie soda has no calories, while sugar and cream add hundreds. It's clear sailing for healthy eating now since the fourth of July is safely behind me."

He regarded her with a quizzical frown. "The fourth of July is a problem?"

"If you love hot dogs, hamburgers, and potato salad." She

extended her hand. "Introductions are a little late, but I'm Penelope Reid."

"Jacob." He shook her hand. His fingers were strong. She wondered what he did for a living—his all-consuming profession. Perhaps he was a professor of some sort—teaching psychology courses or counseling. He projected an air of professionalism, despite his casual appearance.

"Here's to the next holiday, Penelope."

"And will-power." She slipped her hand from his. "Fortunately, there are no holidays until my birthday in November."

Her fiftieth birthday. She left that noteworthy detail out, although she guessed this guy's age close to hers. A few threads of silver in his dark-brown hair caught a sliver of sunlight, and subtle lines were etched on his forehead. Men's ages were often difficult to determine. Many men grew handsomer with age. Jacob was apparently one of them.

"What kind of cake do you like?" he asked.

She paused. No one had ever posed that question to her before. "Carrot cake is my favorite."

"Me too. With cream cheese frosting?"

She gave a thumbs-up. "The best."

After her birthday, and much worse, came Christmas. These past few years, her saddest memories were at Christmas. She struggled hard not to think about her ex's unexplained absences when he'd begun having his affair. They were lonely. And now, with Evan readying to visit his father in Florida by flying there by himself, the days preceding Christmas would be lonelier still.

In truth, she couldn't wait for the holiday to be over. Silently, she shook her head, guilty about her lack of Christmas spirit.

By the time they landed, she realized she had told him the month of her birthday, her hometown, her parenting situation, and her single status.

When the plane stopped at the terminal, Jacob hoisted her carry-on luggage down from the overhead compartment. All Aussie charm, if Australia was indeed his homeland, and chivalrous to a fault.

He followed behind her as they exited the plane, and a blast of sultry air greeted them. A reminder that summer still held a firm hold on the Carolinas.

"A pleasure meeting you, Penelope Reid," he said.

She met his gaze as they stepped into the bustling terminal. "The feeling is mutual, Jacob."

"Safe travels to Roses."

"Thanks. You, too." For wherever he was going. She slung her handbag over her shoulder and grabbed her carry-on bag.

He walked backwards a few steps. "Penelope?"

"Yes?"

He drew out his cell phone. "May I take your picture?"

"Why?"

"Truth?"

"By all means."

"You're a lovely woman."

She hesitated. "Okay."

"More than okay. Perfect." He snapped a photo and pocketed his phone. "Well, cheerio."

"Goodbye, Jacob."

She watched as he departed. Broad shouldered, he held himself tall, self-assured as he disappeared into the swarm of passengers.

Somewhere in her gut, she regretted the fact she wouldn't see him again.

After two hours of non-stop conversation, admittedly one-sided and except for when he was sleeping, she'd only learned his first name.

CHAPTER 1

hat a way for her son to start the second month of seventh grade.

Penelope studied herself in the tall gold mirror propped in her bedroom. She'd dressed professionally—a bohemian style midi dress and strappy sandals, because she planned to head to work after seeing to Evan.

She suspected he had strep throat. Again. What twelve-year-old boy got strep throat every other week?

She'd been surprised the previous evening when he hadn't finished the chocolate ice cream she'd brought to soothe his throat. She'd finished it instead because she couldn't let the ice cream go to waste. She'd used a clean spoon, assuring herself that whatever virus he had wasn't contagious.

"I'm not sick, Mom. Everyone gets sore throats." Evan stood in the living room of their eighteenth-century Victorian home wearing his customary saggy jeans. He shrugged on his black leather jacket. His cheeks shone a bright red, a sprinkling of freckles across his nose. His sturdy build reminded Penelope of herself, though his legs were too long for his body—a promise—if her ex's height was any indication, of the tall man Evan would someday become.

Her thoughts swerved to Jacob and his muscular, sturdy physique. She scolded herself to stop thinking about him—yet he remained in her thoughts. He was a curve in the road, a curve in her life she could ill afford. She didn't know why she'd told him so much about herself.

"Did you hear me, Mom?" Her son interrupted her musings.

The humidity of a Southern October afternoon should have deterred him from wearing a jacket. And what was it about dark colors these days? A kind of rebellion, she supposed. She kept her opinions to herself. No use fighting over small battles like a black jacket.

She placed her hand on his warm forehead. "You have a fever."

He pulled back as if she'd branded him with her touch. Where had her apple-cheeked, angelic son gone? Once Evan hit twelve years old, he'd turned into a mini monster.

"Are you driving me to the doctor's office?" he asked.

Did he try to avoid being seen with her, or was this all her imagination? He sure didn't act like a kid who wanted to go places with his mother. "We can't walk from the outskirts of town. Besides, my throat is sore, too."

"You made two appointments?" He groaned. "We'll be there forever."

"Just one. I'm hoping the doctor will recommend an over-the-counter medicine."

"I'll ask him for you." Evan jutted out his chin in defiance. "Then I can go by myself."

"Dr. Williams' office is past the Roses' recreation center." She vacillated, remembering the numerous swim meets Evan had once participated in.

"So?"

"You used to love to swim." Happy memories flooded her thoughts. "The coach said you were a natural at the butterfly stroke."

"I guess the butterflies flew away," Evan muttered.

"Swimming is a lifelong sport. Exercise builds endurance and will keep you healthy and slim." That last bit slipped out, and her son frowned. She hadn't meant any inference to his weight gain over the past year.

"I like ocean swimming," he said quietly. "The rec center's indoor pool is too closed in."

She wondered how their conversation had gone from strep throat to swimming, but a dialogue, any dialogue, with Evan, was welcome.

"We never lived near the ocean, but we'll visit during the summer." A thought came to mind; overseeing the Hilton Head toy headquarters instead of the shop in Roses, commuting if she was needed in the office. "I'll homeschool you next semester and we can live on Uncle Lincoln's houseboat."

"How will I be able to spend spring break with Dad and Victoria?"

"Your stepmother will be absorbed with the newborn baby, and I'm sure your father and I can work out a congenial solution."

"Oh, right. Like that would ever happen."

A solution might be possible, if her ex was even remotely agreeable, and they didn't get into an argument whenever they discussed custody. Only Roy would move clear to another state to please his young wife, forsaking the needs of his son.

"A houseboat in a harbor is a fishbowl, like living here," Evan said.

"Well, we can rent a cottage farther out. How about Daufuskie? The island is only a short ferry ride from

Hilton Head's mainland and surrounded by the Atlantic Ocean."

"Oh, great. Then everyone at school will call me a freak."

She sighed. There was no pleasing Evan, though she tried and tried. "You're a freak for living on a houseboat?"

"For being home schooled."

She faltered. "Have your classmates called you a freak before?"

"Try every day, Mom. I just want to swim where no one is staring at me. Especially my teammates from the swim team."

"Why on earth would they stare at you?"

"Because I'm fat and ugly and a slow swimmer."

"That's ridiculous."

"Don't say it's not true, because we both know it is. The popular kids don't want anything to do with me." His shoulders hunched, yet his gaze was astute. "You competed in championship competitions. Uncle Lincoln showed me the newspaper clipping when you won first place in freestyle."

"Perseverance pays off."

"You always say swimming is a lifetime sport, but you never swim anymore."

That was her life eons ago, before her college years, her failed marriage. In high school, she'd immersed herself in competitions.

Her life had changed after her marriage.

But not at first. Blissful happiness came first.

And then she'd begun to suspect her husband was unfaithful, though Roy had denied her suspicions. If she ignored the signs, perhaps his affair would go away, she told herself.

It hadn't.

Since the betrayal, heartbreak, and subsequent divorce, she'd fortified herself with an impenetrable barricade. She was serene and no-nonsense. In her youth, she'd been known for her sense of humor, but hardly anything made her laugh anymore.

She breathed in. Nothing was going to topple her hard-earned and sensible equilibrium.

She recalled the comradery with her teammates and the late-night swim meets. She loved belonging to a tight-knit group of friends she relied on. Was Evan missing out on those same memories because he'd abruptly quit the team?

Why hadn't she realized his withdrawal from all extracurricular activities since her divorce and their move to Roses? The signs were clearly there if she'd only taken the time to notice.

You're a bad mom, her conscience reprimanded.

I try my best.

Still, she should've encouraged him more. Instead, she'd become more involved in the business and neglected her son in the bargain.

She took in Evan's appearance—sandy-brown hair and vivid blue eyes, and her heart squeezed. His solid build would thin out as he grew, and his resemblance to her good-looking brother, Lincoln, was striking. Someday, Evan would become a young man with more girlfriends than he could count.

He wasn't aware of that yet and didn't care. He was interested in the present. She prided herself on identifying issues at the toy shop and fixing them. Now she needed to focus on her vulnerable son and fix whatever was causing his problems. She hoped she wasn't too late.

"Make sure your hamster's cage is secure," she said. "Yesterday, he got out and ran all over the house."

"Giblet is a girl, Mom," Evan replied. "Besides, I want a puppy."

"Let's see how well you care for your hamster first. Last week I rescued her from behind a shelf where she got stuck."

Evan obeyed while muttering under his breath for having to do chores when he was sick, and they walked out the front door.

"Won't you be late for work?" he asked.

"Are you still trying to get rid of me?"

He stooped to pick up a loose stone and sent it hurtling across the lawn. "Maybe."

"It hurts when you speak to me like that."

"Sorry, Mom," he muttered.

"I phoned Uncle Lincoln and told him to expect me by midmorning." Penelope kept her voice calm. "He and the staff can easily handle my absence. Besides, I make my own hours."

Penelope and Lincoln shared ownership of New Beginnings Toys, a well-known toy company noted for producing heirloom wooden rocking horses and organic toys. In addition to the Roses shop and headquarters on Hilton Head, the business distributed toys across the United States. Her flight to Virginia had been to finalize the acquisition of another property for expansion.

Since the plane trip, she'd pushed aside her confession to Jacob that she hated her job. Just keep on living and working in a no longer challenging career, was her motto. She led an isolated life, the fate of soon turning fifty, and had come to accept the sad truth.

As a pastime, she'd begun making wooden dolls that children seemed to love, but the craft, though easy and enjoyable, was time-consuming.

"I'll be late for school," Evan said.

"All this concern about lateness. You don't even like school," she said.

Throughout his elementary days, Evan had aced classes and scored straight A report cards. The past couple of years, his grades had slipped. He had no friends, at least none who

18

came over to their house anymore. He stayed in his room, munching on bags of potato chips, and played video games for hours.

Her once athletic son.

"I'll get behind in school if I don't go," he protested. A last-ditch effort, she supposed.

"You'll catch up. This is the only appointment available with the new doctor in town. Emphasis on the word new. Everyone is raving about how gentle and patient he is. The mothers at your school say he's excellent with kids and won't rush us. He'll answer all our questions."

"You mean *my* questions, Mom, not *our*. The appointment is mine. I'm not a kid anymore."

True. He was turning into an adolescent, and she doubted she could live through the next few years.

"Why aren't we seeing Dr. Damian?" Evan asked as he slipped into the front seat of their truck and buckled his seat belt. "I'm used to him."

"For one thing, Uncle Lincoln and I remember Dr. Damian treating us, which goes back decades. For another, Dr. Damian has thankfully retired. I was beginning to question whether he was thorough enough."

"I liked him."

"I was comfortable with him, too. However, I assume Dr. Williams is up on the latest medical techniques."

"Aunt Shanice said he is good-looking."

Shanice was Lincoln's wife. They'd been wed a few years and still displayed a delightful newlywed affection for each other.

Penelope grinned. She'd heard an earful about the handsome Dr. Williams, but romance was the last thing on her mind. He was probably fresh out of medical school, married, with a couple of kids.

When she found a spot in the crowded parking lot, she

parked a distance from the entrance, declaring the walk was beneficial for both her and Evan.

Once they stepped inside the office, the receptionist, clearly flustered, greeted them with a distracted hello and ushered them to a packed waiting room.

"We're behind at least forty-five minutes," she explained. "Dr. Williams was called in for an emergency at the free clinic he established in town. He has returned and is seeing patients, and we apologize for the delay."

Considering the time, Penelope surmised that Dr. Williams kept early hours. Unlike her. She was the opposite of a morning person.

She'd read about the clinic. He'd secured a donated warehouse facility near the hospital and solicited donations from businesses and additional funding through a state grant. He provided free health care to patients who couldn't afford otherwise. Open on weekdays and weekends, the word was spreading, and evening hours were being extended.

After filing their paperwork, the nurse called Evan's name.

Penelope stood, and Evan stuffed his hands into his pockets. Much to Evan's frowning dismay, she followed him into the examining room.

She pointed to her throat, her excuse to accompany him. "You'll get the swab done and tested, and we'll leave with a prescription for your antibiotics in hand. Couldn't be easier."

CHAPTER 2

*E*van plunked onto the examination table and yanked his phone from his pocket.

"Why are you constantly absorbed with your cell phone?" Penelope seated herself on an empty chair across from him.

"Everything is on the internet, Mom. Everyone famous, and whatever is going on in the world."

Penelope pulled out her own cell phone and gestured toward the window. "Isn't the world happening outside and all around us? Your screen doesn't tell the truth."

"You're on *your* phone."

"I intend to get some work done."

He stared straight ahead, his features impassive. "Then why are you always watching me?"

"I don't mean to. I'm worried about you."

"I've had strep throat four times."

"Exactly." In fact, her nerves were frayed. Evan had never been a sickly child, but this year, things were different, beginning with his unhealthy diet. She vowed to make changes in her grocery shopping and eliminate the candy and chips they'd both grown so fond of.

21

The door opened abruptly, and Penelope reminded Evan to put his phone away.

"G' day, mate. Evan, is it?" A tall man stepped inside, his deep male greeting filling the tiny room.

His voice. That accent. She'd recognize him anywhere.

Penelope snapped her phone shut and slowly rose to her feet. An email she'd been typing to an employee was halted in midsentence.

Evan swung his legs back and forth, clearly impatient, still wearing his black leather jacket. He glanced up from the latest video on his phone, a tower defense game he'd tried to explain to her once. At her stern frown and second sharp reminder, he shoved the phone into his pocket.

"I'm Dr. Williams." This attractive doctor, wearing a white coat and khaki pants, exuded competence as he closed the door behind him. A stethoscope hung from around his neck. He looked up from the chart on his clipboard, gave Evan a sincere smile, then turned to Penelope.

Her heart did a double flip.

"You. Here?" she asked.

A beat of silence passed.

"Penelope Reid." He smiled. "I recognized the last name."

"What are you doing in Roses?" She found herself staring. Why couldn't she shake off this attraction to him? Since they'd met on the plane, she continued to envision his slow, discerning smile. His voice had been gentle when he'd leaned close and assured her that he didn't mind her babbling.

He set down the chart. "I bought the practice from Dr. Damian."

"I thought you preferred big cities."

"I changed my mind."

Whoa. Not because of her. No, of course not.

"You never mentioned anything on the plane," she said.

"What plane?" Evan asked.

22

"Dr. Williams and I met a while ago when I ... we ... flew back from Virginia."

"I visited several physicians' practices before making my final decision." Jacob studied her. "I interviewed in Virginia, then planned to fly on to Florida. I made a detour in Hilton Head."

"A detour," she echoed. "To Roses. You never mentioned any interviews."

Why would an older doctor buy another doctor's practice? Had Jacob lost his own practice due to incompetence?

He offered a half smile. "I believe you did most of the talking on the plane."

He was hardly the young, recently out-of-medical school doctor she'd anticipated.

He turned to Evan, who assessed their conversation with a peculiar, thoughtful scowl.

"Anything you'd like to talk to me about, Evan?" Jacob asked. "How's it hangin'?"

"My throat hurts."

"You're how old?" Jacob scanned Evan's chart.

"I'm twelve."

"Almost an adult, mate. Shall we ask your mum to leave?"

"No." Evan shot a glance toward Penelope. "She can stay. She has a sore throat, too."

"I'm fine." She waved off his remark. She didn't want to discuss any illness of hers with Jacob Williams. She intended to keep her replies brief and avoid any personal connection. "My sore throat went away."

"Did it?" Jacob pressed the back of his hand to her forehead. His touch was warm and firm. Her cheeks heated.

"She wants you to recommend an over-the-counter medicine for her," Evan chimed in.

Jacob quirked an eyebrow. "Does she now?"

"If a recommendation isn't too much trouble," she said.

23

Jacob dropped his hand. "No trouble at all. Let's have a look at your son first." He lifted his stethoscope and listened to Evan's heart and lungs. "Nothing of concern there." He flipped a page on his chart and made a note. Then he produced a swab and instructed Evan to say "ah." Much to Penelope's surprise, Evan didn't gag. His usual sullen expression vanished. In fact, he urged Jacob to explain the test.

"Evan is tossing around becoming a physician or a veterinarian when he gets older," Penelope explained.

Evan crossed his arms. "I want a puppy."

"Do you like dogs?" Jacob asked.

"I love dogs."

"Is that why you're interested in becoming a vet?"

Evan shrugged. "Maybe."

"I'm encouraging him." Penelope turned to Jacob. "What mother doesn't hope her son will someday become a doctor?"

"I can name one." Jacob looked away before meeting her gaze. "You're a sweet and caring mum, Penelope Reid."

"I don't know about the sweet part." Evan was scowling at her again. Flustered, she groped for a subject change. "Evan loves all animals."

People ... well, not so much.

"The medical profession needs bright young minds," Jacob said.

They returned to the waiting room while awaiting the results, then were summoned back to the examining room. As Penelope suspected, the test confirmed strep throat.

Evan's eyes widened. "I've got strep for the fifth time?"

"You're obviously susceptible to strep," she replied. "Does your throat still hurt?"

"Are you kidding? Yes."

She turned to Jacob. "Our previous doctor recommended a tonsillectomy for Evan."

"Weigh the pros and cons of a tonsillectomy at Evan's age," Jacob said. "There's always a risk of complications from the surgery. A recent study suggests patients are more prone to long-term respiratory disease afterwards."

"I don't want an operation," Evan said.

"I agree, at least for now." Jacob extended a hand to Evan and shook. "Have a good one. I'll send a prescription for antibiotics to the local pharmacy, and you should start feeling better in two or three days. And this is my recommendation for your mom." He scribbled on a sheet of paper and handed it to her.

She scanned the instructions. "Tea with honey and lemon and loads of rest?"

"Works like a charm."

"When should Evan return to school?"

"I'd advise he stay home for at least forty-eight hours after he starts the antibiotics."

"Good," Evan said. "If I don't ever have to go to school again, my life will be a lot better."

"Quitting isn't an option, Evan," she broke in. "You'll never be a doctor if you can't finish junior high."

Evan opened his mouth.

The last thing she needed was her son spilling more of their personal affairs. Jacob Williams knew enough about her already.

She cut Evan off with an abrupt nod.

"Thank you, Doctor," she said.

"Please call me Jacob."

She felt torn. She really wanted to keep up the formality in a doctor's office, but she really, really liked calling Jacob by his first name.

She nodded. "Okay."

"Thanks, Dr. Jacob," Evan chimed in.

"Not you," she replied. "To you, he's Dr. Williams."

"Why? That's not fair."

"Life isn't always fair. We're adults. You're a kid, and you must be respectful."

"Why would your life be better if you didn't attend school?" Jacob's gaze swayed to Evan.

"Because all the kids hate me, and I hate them."

"I could use some help in my clinic. Do you ever volunteer?"

Evan lifted his shoulders. "Not much, unless I go with my mom."

"Oh, where do you go?"

"She and Uncle Lincoln donate toys to the homeless center in town."

"Several of the families I see are refugees from other countries," Jacob said. "They come into my clinic for free health care."

"We hang out with the kids at the shelter and help them with homework and stuff," Evan continued. "Mom was bringing in the wooden dolls she made, but not anymore."

"I'm tied up at work," she murmured.

"Admirable, and very creative. I encourage you to get back to it." Jacob shot Penelope an approving glance, then turned to Evan. "Would you like to lend a hand in the clinic, mate?"

Evan fixed his gaze on the tile floor. "Doing what?"

"Whatever the moment requires because the patients' needs change minute by minute. How are your phone skills?"

"Okay."

"We need more beds and chairs. I'll give you a list of the other clinics in the area," Jacob said. "Do you speak Spanish?"

"He doesn't, but Evan took a signing class last year," Penelope put in.

"I'm in seventh grade." Evan rolled his eyes. "I can communicate all by myself, Mom."

Jacob concentrated on Evan. "Signing will be helpful for my deaf patients."

"Okay," Evan mumbled.

Penelope's eyebrows raised. *I can't believe my son agreed so easily.*

"Excellent." Jacob patted Evan on the back, and she caught Jacob's smirk as he winked at her. "I'll ask the nurse to provide the details. She volunteers at the clinic every Saturday morning. Will Saturday work for you, Evan?"

"I guess."

"Can you arrive by seven?"

Evan blinked. "A.M.?"

"Yep."

"Evan doesn't usually get up until—" Penelope tried to keep her voice neutral.

Jacob made eye contact with her and gave a subtle shake of his head.

His silent message, to allow Evan to answer for himself, stopped her. She knew what Jacob surmised. She was an overprotective, hovering parent.

Evan broke the ensuing silence. "All right. I'll get up early."

"Let's plan on a week from this upcoming Saturday, so you have several days to recuperate."

As they exited, Penelope's chest filled with encouragement over the conversation. Jacob Williams had accomplished a great deal during their short office visit. Whether he realized or not, and she had a sneaking suspicion he did, he'd given her son a purpose.

At the pharmacy, Evan waited in the car. Penelope hastened inside and collided with Candee Winchester, a local realtor. Candee was a striking woman with wavy auburn hair and an amiable personality. She'd married Teddy, one of her clients and a real estate investor. They'd adopted his nephew, Joseph, who loved horses.

"What brings you to the pharmacy on a weekday morning?" Candee slung her handbag over her shoulder and juggled a bag filled with cleaning supplies. She explained that she and Teddy were redoing her office.

"I'm picking up a prescription for Evan," Penelope said. "He has strep throat again."

"Did you see the handsome new doctor?"

"The guy everyone is fixated on?"

"Who else?" Candee had made a name for herself as the town matchmaker, and Penelope recognized her cupid grin from a mile away. "I'm working to find him a house here. In the meantime, he's renting an apartment at the old Roses Hotel."

"Lincoln never mentioned anything."

Lincoln and Penelope had purchased the rundown hotel and renovated it. Besides an investment, the hotel provided housing for their toy shop employees. A couple of years ago, though, they'd sold the hotel, preferring to concentrate on their business rather than real estate.

"I've shown Dr. Williams numerous properties, though he's very particular." Candee fingered the gold cross earrings she always wore. "He wants what he wants, all wrapped up in a certain low-price range."

"I assumed a doctor's salary was more than ample."

"For whatever reason, not in his case."

Penelope picked up the prescription. Before she headed out the door, she bought three chocolate candy bars. She earned them, she decided, foreseeing a challenging week ahead while caring for her cranky son.

CHAPTER 3

The following day, Jacob grinned at the remembrance of his brief conversation with Penelope and her son in his office. He'd never met a teen who liked to get up early, and Evan proved no exception. He admired the boy's commitment when agreeing to volunteer at the clinic. Of course, the real test was yet to come. Would Evan show up at the assigned hour?

Jacob scanned his mile-long to-do list for the evening. More house-hunting with Candee Winchester can wait, he concluded, as he closed his office.

He looked up Penelope's address, discovered she lived on the edge of town, and decided to drive to her home. He'd purchased a ten-year-old yellow four-door Volkswagen when he'd moved to Roses. Driving wasn't his thing, and he'd never gotten used to seeing cars on the wrong side of the road in America. He'd relied on big-city transportation in Atlanta, and Roses didn't boast subways. Fortunately, traffic here was minimal.

He didn't make house calls, and strep throat wasn't usually a cause for concern. However, Evan was a new patient, and, for lack of any other reason, rational or otherwise, why not? He was attracted to Penelope and wanted to get to know her better.

Reservations stirred. He'd vowed to keep his life simple ever since his niece's death. He'd vowed to prioritize what was important. He'd vowed to devote his career to serving people.

Eighteen-hour workdays had worked well throughout his successful career. He had shouldered all responsibility with unrestrained energy, though he had never achieved his goal.

Success and kudos aren't necessary anymore, he reminded himself.

He'd quit his job; walked away to reassess and refocus, searching for more simplistic goals.

His thoughts gravitated to Penelope.

From what he'd learned from their plane conversation, she was anything but simple. However, she was unassuming and vivacious. In fact, she was a stunner.

Penelope revealed that Evan's father didn't see his son much anymore. Although he didn't intend to become a surrogate father, Jacob made a mental note to engage with Evan, and volunteering at the clinic proved a positive beginning.

He located Penelope's home and parked at the curb, viewing the expansive driveway, and surrounding half acre of land. Inhaling, he breathed in freshly mowed grass and the honeyed scent of late-blooming flowers.

Her home was a beaut. A splendid, old-fashioned Victorian, classic, with a rectangular shaped, sloping roof, and boasting a veranda.

He got out of his car and scanned the property. This was the house he envisioned for himself. This was exactly the type of house he was looking for.

The few Candee had shown him were out of his price

range. He'd poured a lot of money into helping his sister, Kylie, rebuild her life after his niece's death, and even more money setting up his clinic.

He paused to study Penelope's home. He wasn't certain what to expect when he stepped inside, but based on the exterior, he assumed the interior was gorgeous.

All the homes he'd viewed in Roses had lacked one specific requirement. He wanted to have a medical practice in his home, and most weren't big enough. This home, painted in colors of vivid blue with gold trim, resembled a doll house. Standing two stories, with a stained-glass window facing the street and a rounded turret, the architecture was a reminder of the historic Victorian era, where nothing came cheap.

He surveyed the area. The house was located at the end of a main road leading to town.

Penelope hadn't exaggerated when she'd described Roses. Storybook wasn't an adequate description. The town was idyllic, a scene straight out of a Norman Rockwell painting. In addition, from his early morning jogs, he'd discovered something even better than a wholesome culture. He'd observed the heart.

The people.

Young and old alike were kind, interested in others, and respectful. Honest and polite and middle America at its best, where church was at the center.

He scanned the block. Other homes and businesses were located nearby Penelope's house. Surely the area was zoned for both business and residential properties.

Not only would a home office reduce his overhead, but he could treat more patients on evenings and weekends. He liked the idea of a short commute from his kitchen to his office instead of driving to town.

Trouble was, this house was hers, not his.

You'll never be able to afford anything on this scale. Occasionally, his mother's voice echoed in his ears, and his chest tightened. He allowed the mental numbness to take hold and shook away his contemplation.

He *could* afford a lovely home.

Eventually.

He stepped onto the porch. After seeing patients at his office all day, he'd stopped at his rental apartment at the Roses Hotel to shower and change into dark jeans and a clean T-shirt.

He rang the doorbell. From inside, a squeal sounded.

"Giblet, get into your cage this instant." The sound of rushing footsteps. "There, I've got you. Come with me, it's probably the postman with a late toy delivery." She opened the front door with a tiny hamster nestled in her hands.

She gaped. "Jacob?"

"Hello, Penelope." He caught his breath. He'd forgotten what she'd been wearing on the plane, or in his office, but it wasn't a stunning striped dress that flared at the waist.

That generous figure. Her bare toes peeked out from a pair of beige sandals. He'd be thinking about her for the rest of the evening. Oddly, her sharp blue eyes, focused on him, were even more captivating.

Her gaze narrowed. "Why are you here?"

"I'm not delivering any toys."

"I can see that. Is Evan supposed to report to your clinic tonight?"

"I hope not, unless he intended to expose my patients to strep throat."

"Then why?" A slight breeze lifted her dark hair, shaped in a short bob style. Classy and elegant silver highlights framed her round face. He wanted to tuck one of the stray strands behind her ears. He wanted—

He cleared his throat. "You drink coffee, right?"

"Every day."

He held out a bag of ground coffee he'd picked up at the local shop in town. "Did you reach your quota for today?"

"That will never happen."

"Care to brew us a cup?"

Fearing she might protest, he held up a hand to hold her off.

"You like coffee, too?" she asked.

"Very much." He had her compete attention.

"You didn't mention anything about coffee on the plane."

"No?"

Her delicate eyebrows came together. "All you said was that you liked to drink."

"I do, especially ginger beer."

She tilted her head. "What is ginger beer?"

"A beverage made from ginger, sugar, and water."

"Is the beer alcoholic?"

"Sometimes. Where I come from, ginger beer is a local favorite."

"Australia?"

"Yea. Down under."

"I suspected you were from Australia but couldn't place your accent for certain." She peered out the door. "You drove here?"

"I didn't ride my kangaroo. In fact, riding a kangaroo is forbidden in Australia."

"Probably in America, too."

"Why did you suspect I was Australian?"

She offered a half-smile. "Your accent is a dead giveaway."

"I've never been able to shake it."

"You've lived in America a long time?"

He stroked his fingers over the hamster's caramel-colored fur. "Uh-huh."

"A man's foreign accent is usually appealing to a woman." She stared at him while holding the wriggling hamster.

"Usually?"

She didn't reply and pushed the door open wider with her hip. "Would you like to come in?"

"I was hoping you'd ask."

"I don't have any ginger beer."

He shook the bag. "I'll provide the coffee."

She ushered him inside and cradled the hamster. "Are you afraid of hamsters?"

"Is he going to race about?"

"Not if I can help it, and I've been informed that Giblet is a she. Evan refilled her water bowl a while ago and didn't secure the cage." Penelope placed the hamster in a cage situated on a table in the hallway and secured the latch. "Are you comfortable with animals?"

"Animals are my passion." Jacob closed the door behind him. The gorgeous Penelope was becoming his passion, too. "My family owned a dog, a golden retriever."

"In Australia?"

"We moved to the States when I entered primary school and gave the dog to a friend. My mum and dad announced that our dog was too old for a big trip and a bigger change."

"Didn't your parents like Australia?"

"Australia is awesome, from what I remembered, and they both grew up near Melbourne, where I was raised. Unfortunately, my father went bankrupt."

"I'm sorry," she said quietly.

He shifted. Alrighty, then. If he was trying to make a good impression, blurting out his family's descent into poverty wasn't the best way to go about it.

"We struggled, but we landed on our feet," he replied.

"What happened?"

"The bankruptcy? Long story. My father packed up my

mum, my sister, Kylie, and me and then found a job in Maryland. We've lived in the States ever since."

"Do you see your parents often?"

"My mum, on occasion. My sister lives near her but is considering moving back to Australia."

"Do you visit your mother?"

"Not as often as I should."

"Is your sister older or younger?"

"Kylie is younger than me. She and her husband split soon after …" He swallowed the lump in his throat. The expected tears came to his eyes.

Penelope studied him, giving him no place to look but straight at her. She didn't press him for any more details, and he didn't offer an explanation.

"I'm sorry," she said simply.

"Thanks." He couldn't say more. After a difficult and uncomfortable minute with no words, he relaxed. That was extraordinary. He never relaxed when he spoke about his adorable niece, Linda, and her tragic death. Normally, he tensed and felt worse.

"If you ever need to talk with someone." Penelope offered a tentative smile. "I'm a good listener. I don't usually babble on and on. Honest." She attempted to lighten the mood with a disparaging wave at herself. She'd noted his sadness and responded with empathy.

He moved from one foot to the other. "I won't be discussing the subject again but thank you."

"I talked nonstop on the plane."

He couldn't help his smile. Quiet filled the air, spun with kindness and understanding. He recognized the whiff of lavender, her scent.

"I liked your stories." He kept his expression neutral. "Do you want to hear a truth?"

"This truth business again?" Her lips twitched. "Sure."

"You're a remarkable woman." His observation surprised himself. He truly was interested in her. In fact, he planned to learn everything about her.

He surveyed the expansive living room, the cushioned window seat overlooking the side yard. A cherry-wood coffee table and armchairs were cluttered with books. People called him a neatnik. Maybe so. He pressed down the inclination to straighten the stacks, so all the book edges aligned.

"Gorgeous home." He peered up at the high ceilings, the gold-carved wooden mirror hanging over the marble fireplace. The room was painted a rich hue of chocolate brown. He assumed to his left was the music room, judging by the ebony-black grand piano. No white or beige walls anywhere.

"You play piano?" he asked.

"I tried. I struggled. I couldn't get the hang of reading the notes in the bass clef, so I quit."

"On the plane, you mentioned you wanted to create something."

The corners of her eyes crinkled. "If you ask my piano teacher, she'll assure you it wasn't a Mozart sonata."

He gestured toward the wooden beads, paint, sharpies, newspaper, and glue on a separate table. Several beads were painted in various neutral shades and stood upright. "Are these the dolls you're making?"

She shrugged. "I've put the craft aside."

He stepped into the room and picked up a miniature doll. Her black hair and blue eyes were intricately drawn, her hands clasped together. Two yellow silk hair bows were glued on either side of her head above her ears.

"She is precious." He fingered the hair bows.

"I name all my dolls after spices. Hers is Cinnamon."

"Nice name."

"Our business has a large amount of scrap wood I can use."

"Right." He'd looked up her toy shop on the internet.

"I brought the dolls to the homeless shelter Evan mentioned. My brother Lincoln donated several rocking horses, but I decided each child needed something simple."

Simple. There was that word again.

"Congrats on a worthwhile project," he said. "I'm learning simple is best."

"Me too. Life is all about balance. So many material things are relatively useless."

"Like big expensive cars."

She grinned. "And designer purses."

"You're an inspiration, Penelope."

She picked up a tiny blue silk scarf and handed it to him. "I love this craft. Of course, you're familiar with my story."

"Some parts. Remember, I'm an excellent listener, so keep talking."

"When you're not sleeping," she reminded. "I prefer to keep my story to the parts you've probably memorized, so don't press me, okay?"

"Apologies." He draped the tiny scarf over the doll's shoulders. "Sometimes I lose my finesse around beautiful women. Women who have survived hardships and heartbreak are even more …"

She snatched the doll from him, readjusting the scarf before setting the doll back on the table. "You should've stopped when you were ahead with the word 'beautiful.'"

"You're also fun and creative."

"I'll brew your coffee, and you can tell me the reason you're here." She breezed down the hallway, and he followed. The wooden floor creaked as they stepped into the kitchen.

"I dropped by to see Evan," Jacob said. "How is he feeling?"

"So, this is a house call?"

Truth? Well, he wasn't ready for the blatant truth, because he hadn't come to terms with it yet himself.

"You can call it a house call," he replied.

"Evan is resting." Penelope surveyed the hallway, as if Evan might materialize at any moment. "Correction. He's playing video games. Do you want to go upstairs and check on him?"

"You're his mum." Jacob moved beside her. "What do you suggest?"

"Stay down here." She nudged him, a lighthearted nudge. "He'd probably prefer to run a 5K race than see you. He's a bit prickly when he's interrogated." Though she joked, her face beamed whenever she mentioned her son. Her delight exposed a wide-open fracture in his own defenses and his attraction to her. Again, he questioned himself. What was he really doing here?

"I blame his change in disposition on the rough road to adolescence," she finished.

When she opened the bag, Jacob inhaled the scent of fresh ground coffee.

"Is the antibiotic working?" he asked.

"Antibiotics are a miracle drug." She scrutinized him, peeling away more and more layers of his resistance. "You realize, Jacob, that not many doctors make personal house calls anymore."

"I'm new in town." Same old excuse, and he debated whether he should elaborate. "This is a way for me to get to know my patients better."

"Do you make calls often?"

"Not very often." In fact, he never had.

She spooned four scoops of coffee, then measured filtered water into the coffeepot. "Your interest means a lot. Most physicians won't take the time."

"My patients are the reason I'm a doctor."

"You look like a doctor." She switched on the coffee machine, then appraised him from head to toe. "I should've realized that on the plane. I imagined you—"

He stepped closer to the counter. Why was he so fascinated with her?

A difficult remembrance of his marriage and subsequent divorce resurfaced.

"I'm having a baby," his wife, Janet, had declared. Tears had poured down her cheeks. He'd assumed they were tears of joy, and he joined in with ecstatic tears of his own. Before he could bring out the champagne glasses, she'd added, "The baby isn't yours." And thus, the marriage had ended.

Her unfaithfulness had killed his pride and left him stunned.

"Where did you go, Doctor?" Penelope's steady voice drew him back from the devastating remembrance.

"Down memory lane," he said.

"Joyful times?"

He tapped his chin. "No. I was thinking about my ex-wife."

"You mentioned you were married."

"A decade ago, and for a couple of years. She's an anchorwoman on a national network. You'd probably recognize her. In fact, she was awarded an honor for investigative journalism."

"I'm impressed."

"Don't be." He blinked. "Let's discuss something else. You were in the middle of imagining me."

"I'd like to hear more about you."

He'd severed all recollections of Janet from his mind, though when he caught a glimpse of her on a cable television show, a slight pinch of awareness went through him. Thankfully, nothing more. He'd made peace with the hurt she'd caused and resolved never to get his heart all twisted up

39

again. He dated women casually, and the women knew not to demand any emotional entanglement from him.

So, for the umpteenth bloody time, what on earth was he doing in Penelope's kitchen?

As a concerned physician, I'm here for Evan.

"I'm a doctor," he said aloud.

"At first, I imagined you as a professor who worked in academia."

"Why?"

"You cited statistics about airplanes."

He stepped back as she reached around him to grab two mugs from a high glass cabinet. She handed them to him, one by one.

He set the mugs on the wooden kitchen table. "A single offhand remark, and you pegged me as Professor Jacob."

"Now that I think of it, you don't fit the stereotype."

"Which is?"

"Shirt, tie, and tweed jacket."

"Another cliché." He folded cloth napkins she handed him and placed the napkins next to the mugs. "Are you interested in how I pictured you, Penelope?"

"After we went our separate ways?"

"While you were working at your job."

"Probably sitting on the floor and playing with tiny toy trucks."

"Gorgeous blue eyes, brown hair, and drop-dead gorgeous." He followed her back to the counter and grabbed two spoons. "I checked your website and saw your photo. You own New Beginnings Toys."

"The photo is old." She pushed back her hair, the hint of silver strands. Her cheeks turned crimson. "How did you realize I was one of the owners of the toy shop?"

"I asked Candee to verify for certain. The custom, hand-made rocking horses are ..."

"Our specialty."

"Right. And now you can sell your charming wooden dolls there."

"Hardly a specialty, and I don't sell them. If I had my way, I'd gift them to every child in the world." Her gaze shifted to the stairway. "Evan is returning to school in a couple of days. He's not thrilled about going back."

"Why doesn't he like school?"

"Peer pressure. Twelve years old is a challenging age." She placed sugar and a creamer on the table and poured steaming coffee into two mugs. Once she sat, he claimed the chair across from her.

"I met one of Evan's friends at the office today," he said. "He came in for a checkup."

"Oh?"

"A polite kid named Zack. He mentioned he was in seventh grade, and I asked him if he knew Evan."

"Zack was once Evan's best friend."

"Not anymore?"

She cupped her hands around her mug. "Not anymore."

"Zack inquired about volunteering at the clinic, and I encouraged him. He seems an ambitious chap. He is trying out for the high school swim team." Jacob spooned sugar into his coffee and stirred. "The coach accepts students in junior high."

"If the swimmer is good enough. A big *if.*"

"Is Evan trying out?"

"He'd rather wash dinner dishes for a week." Penelope circled the rim of her mug with her forefinger. "A couple of years ago, he was the star of the team. Now he doesn't seem to belong anywhere, and I have no idea how to help him."

Let Evan find his own way. The consideration came to Jacob's mind, and he quickly dismissed it. He had no right to tell Penelope how to raise her child.

41

An hour passed quicker than anticipated—an easy hour, filled with friendly conversation. She discussed the toy business and explained that everything had to be worth the cost of the retail value. Business was business. However, toys were unique and personal to each child. Discerning parents chose specialty toys for their children, believing in the value when cheap plastic toys were readily available at every big box store.

The perfect toy was designed as an heirloom for the child and family, Penelope went on, though she and her brother were businesspeople, and profit was a consideration. Excited parents gushed to their friends that they were being mindful of what they bought for their children, so everyone was satisfied.

Success meant Penelope's employees continued to work, and the toy shops remained open. It also meant that Penelope and her brother could continue to enjoy a comfortable lifestyle.

When Jacob stood, she walked him to the front door. "As usual, I did all the talking."

He smiled. "I always liked making house calls."

Evan never materialized, and Jacob didn't press the issue. After all, Penelope assured him that Evan was getting better.

"Thanks for the coffee," she said.

"You're welcome. I like your home. It's exactly the type of place I'm looking for."

"I met Candee in the pharmacy. If anyone can find your dream house, she's your realtor."

"Considering my hectic schedule," he said, "I've had only a few hours to scope out Roses and the surrounding area, and my house-hunting is hindered."

"I've lived here most of my life."

He knew that from their conversation on the plane.

"Where is the best place to find a home?" he asked. "Any suggestions?"

"Well, I—"

At the doorway, he turned to her. "May I call you?"

"Why? I don't need another prescription. In your professional opinion, I needed tea with honey and lemon and lots of rest."

He grinned with satisfaction and squeezed her hands. "Did my prescription help?"

"The tea is a blessing, though I couldn't manage the 'lots of rest' part."

"Can you show me around the area this weekend? Candee is good, but you're better."

She withdrew her hands and stepped backward. "I'm not a realtor."

"Doesn't matter."

"Evan is sick."

"If he continues to take the antibiotic, he'll make a full recovery by Saturday," Jacob replied. "Perhaps he can stay with your brother and sister-in-law for a bit. They live in Roses, right?"

She looked flustered. "I'm not sure. I suppose I can ask them."

"After I leave the clinic tomorrow, I'll phone you to firm up our plans."

"Phone?"

"Or I'll text you." He asked for her cell phone, texted himself, then handed the phone back to her. "Afterwards, we can go for dinner."

"You mean to eat?"

"You aren't on a diet, are you?"

"I'm trying to choose healthy. Look, this probably isn't a suitable idea."

"Order a salad."

She shook her head. "You're Evan's doctor."

"Are you dating anyone?"

"I told you." Her gaze sharpened. "I gave up dating."

"No pizzerias. I promise."

Her cell phone pinged, and she read the text with a concerned frown. "Sorry, Jacob, I need to contact the supervisor at our Roses location." She tapped a number into her phone. "A shipment is delayed because of stormy weather in New York, and the delay is causing repercussions to our stores along the East Coast. With the holidays approaching soon—"

"No worries. I'll let myself out." As she put the phone to her ear and began instructing the supervisor, Jacob mouthed, "I'll call you."

He closed the front door behind him before she could protest.

Penelope Reid was a remarkable woman. Despite her rather slapdash appearance on the plane, and the untidy state of her house, she was quick, conscientious, and decisive at her job. Too bad it was a job she hated.

CHAPTER 4

*P*enelope didn't know why she'd agreed to Jacob's request, and she dissected their conversation as she pulled into the driveway of Lincoln and Shanice's farmhouse on Saturday.

Shanice had inherited the farmhouse from her grandmother, Jasmine, and the house even had a name—Jasmine's Joy.

Evan had missed the entire week at school, declaring he wasn't feeling well enough to attend, and his accommodating teachers had sent online assignments to him. Penelope hovered over his shoulder, offering to help.

"What a great idea, Mom," Evan said. "As if the teachers won't realize it's your work and not mine."

"I didn't say I would do the work." She reached for the homework papers her son had printed.

"I've got this covered, okay? Science is my favorite subject."

Science had always been her worst subject, so she agreed.

She could only trust that he'd completed the assignments.

"I'm showing Jacob Williams the town of Roses and

45

prospective houses for sale," Penelope began, after Lincoln opened the front door and welcomed her and Evan inside the farmhouse.

Evan disappeared into the living room and dropped his backpack onto the floor. He clicked on the television set, and Penelope heard a delighted squeal when Shanice's cat and Lincoln's dog jumped on the couch beside him.

The couple had no children and frequently discussed adoption. Currently, they devoted their free time to expanding New Beginnings Toys and renovating the rambling farmhouse.

"I think showing him the town is a wonderful idea," Shanice remarked when Penelope stepped into the kitchen.

"He trapped me into this," Penelope replied.

"Trapped is when you're stuck inside for days after a snowstorm. Hanging out with Dr. Handsome is exciting."

"I'm not his realtor," Penelope said. "Besides, I can't choose the right house for him."

Shanice tucked a stand of thick ebony hair behind her ear, then grabbed plates from the glass-fronted cabinet. "For some reason, he prefers you. I wonder why?"

"Short explanation. I'm a native of Roses."

"Honestly, Penny." Shanice referred to Penelope by her nickname. "Jacob is a dream come true. Rumor has it that he's single and in his early fifties. If he wants to spend time with you, don't fight it."

Because you're married to Lincoln, who clearly loves you. You have no fears of denials and infidelity and heartbreak, Penelope thought.

Shanice plated oversized portions of sweet potato pie and carried the plates to the table.

"Jacob Williams moved into town only a short time ago and has already established a free clinic," Shanice said. "He's committed to helping the community and is an exceptional doctor."

"He's interested in his patients," Penelope said. "How many doctors make house calls anymore?"

Shanice smiled conspiratorially at Lincoln, then beamed at Penelope. "None, and certainly not for a case of strep throat. Any ideas on what drew him to visit you?"

"He is new in town."

"We've established that," Shanice replied.

"Okay, he is admired." At her sister-in-law's obvious delight at her statement, Penelope amended, "I like him as a friend."

"He's an eligible bachelor."

"I see where you're headed, and the answer is, I'm not interested. After my nasty divorce, dating is no longer in the cards for me." Penelope forked a piece of pie and smirked at Lincoln. "Are you aware your wife has already married me off to this guy?"

"She's a cheerleader for your happiness. We're both thrilled you opened your life to a man. Give him a chance. You're finally excited about dating someone. With the holidays approaching—"

"Lincoln, we're not dating. You're envisioning Jacob and I under a mistletoe, kissing, and married by New Year's Day." She peered around the expansive kitchen. "You've started to decorate for Christmas. I love the reindeer salt and pepper shakers. And the poinsettias from the garden center are gorgeous, especially the red and pink ones. I noticed them by the fireplace when I walked in."

"And we celebrate Kwanzaa, too." He looked fondly at his wife, then back at Penelope. "Don't you want to spend the holidays with a special someone? You've been alone too long."

"Maybe, sometimes."

"That special someone may be right under your nose." He studied her intently. "You blush whenever his name is mentioned."

Her warm face gave her away. "Jacob is originally from Australia."

"Ooh, I love an Australian man's accent," Shanice said.

Lincoln's eyebrows furrowed. "More than mine?"

"You don't have an accent."

He drummed his fingers on the table. "I have a Southern accent."

"So do I, and that doesn't count because a Southern accent isn't exotic. I've heard it my whole life. However, I love you anyway." Shanice leaned over and kissed him on the cheek. He placed his fork on his plate, pulled her closer, and kissed her back.

Penelope grinned when Shanice broke the kiss. "You two are an inspiration."

Their infectious laughter wafted throughout the kitchen.

Lincoln was Penelope's younger brother—square-jawed, considerate, and generous, and he and Shanice had been granted a second chance when he'd returned to Roses. He'd pursued her, married her, and they planned to raise a family.

When Penelope regarded them, a twinge of longing went through her chest. They'd found each other and enjoyed a loving marriage.

Meanwhile, her ex had cheated on her with another woman—someone decades younger and much prettier.

Jealousy knocked, though not followed by grief. Penelope refused to jump into the courting game again, and she'd declared her decision to everyone who would listen. In her defense, she'd tried dating, both online and in person, and both were unsuccessful.

Shanice shifted her gaze to Penelope. "I can't wait to meet Dr. Williams."

"He's a pediatrician, so I doubt you'll have the opportunity for a while."

"Oh, you'll introduce us well before that." Shanice wiggled her eyebrows. "Seems as if you two are spending oodles of time getting better acquainted."

Penelope leaned back in her chair. "We only spent a few hours together because his visit to my house was a—"

"House call," the husband and wife chorused in unison. "And don't forget the plane. Remember, you told us all about it."

Penelope noted the glints in their eyes and laughed.

"Did the good doctor examine Evan while he was at your house?" Shanice asked. "Water, anyone?" At their nods, she stepped to the refrigerator and grabbed several bottles.

"No, although Jacob inquired about him," Penelope replied, accepting a bottle from Shanice. "We didn't want to bother Evan because he was in his room playing video games."

"Makes perfect sense. Not." Lincoln chuckled. "Either way, we're delighted. Your divorce was difficult, and I ... we ... Shay and I, are pleased you're interested in a good man."

Any mention of Penelope's ex set off a chain of reactions, and she sternly fought to keep her sadness under control. She sliced her pie portion in half and slid the pie onto Lincoln's plate. "My birthday is coming soon," she explained at his quizzical expression. "I've been eyeing a lovely dress, though it's quite short and clingy. My figure could use a remodel."

"Don't shortchange yourself." Shanice placed her hand on Penelope's forearm. "You are beautiful."

"I appreciate you handling the snafu with the shipping problem the other day." Lincoln took a swig of water. "You put in a good deal of effort to solve it. I don't say it often enough, but you are vital to our company's success."

I hate my job. Penelope's words to Jacob echoed in her mind.

However, if she examined her statement, she didn't hate her job. She'd simply grown tired of doing the same tasks day after day, year after year.

Initially, she'd assumed the responsibilities of the family business to please her father. She'd worked at the toy shop throughout high school, and then slipped right back into the business after college.

When had she become indispensable? How could she ever leave when her brother depended on her? Equally important, what would she do instead? She was proficient at organizing, yet not overly adept at shaping her own life.

Her inferiority stemmed from her ex's cheating. A major hit to her self-confidence.

Old news. Old excuses. Look ahead. Refuse to dwell on the past.

"Evan assured me that he finished his science essay, though you may want to double-check," she said. "He brought his backpack, but he won't allow me anywhere near his assignments."

"He only missed a few days of school." Lincoln steepled his fingers together. "He is responsible."

She gazed out the window. A rustic barn was framed in the distance, along with a firepit, and the rolling hills of Roses beyond. "Why won't he let me help him?"

"Because he needs to learn some things by himself. Think how proud he'll feel when he turns in the assignments."

"He hates school. I wish he loved seventh grade as much as I did."

"You loved seventh grade?" Shanice smirked. "I never met anyone who loved seventh grade."

Penelope craned her neck toward the living room and observed her son. He seemed so vulnerable sitting on the couch between the dog and cat. So solitary. Her foolish fear of him failing stemmed from her own difficulties in school, she rationalized. She'd struggled and never been able to achieve the high grades her younger brother attained with ease.

Logically, she knew Lincoln was right, and she was grasping for excuses to hold on to her only child. If only time stood still, or at least slowed down.

She speculated. Had the past year flown by for Evan, as it had for her? Likely, the twelve months had been interminable.

"I want Evan to be confident in himself," she murmured.

"You're doing a fine job raising him," Lincoln said.

Then why didn't Evan have any friends?

Her thoughts tangled. When things weren't right in Evan's world, they weren't right in hers, either.

She wanted him to enjoy the childhood she never had. Her father was a taskmaster who set impossible standards. A workaholic, aiming for success at all costs.

Evan shouldn't be held back because of her—a woman who might never recover from humiliation and hurt caused by sorrow and misgivings.

"He's acting like a preteen," Lincoln said. "He's perfectly normal."

"He's down on himself," she murmured.

"He has gained weight this year," Shanice broke in, then put a hand to her mouth. "I'm sorry. I shouldn't have mentioned anything."

"It's okay." Penelope blew out a breath. "Sometimes I feel helpless. I'm trying to eliminate junk food in the house, although I'm equally guilty. Lately, I've been encouraging him to be more active. He's touchy and snappish if I mention swimming."

"He is welcome to keep us company any time. We have chickens in the barn, a dog, a cat, and more plants than we can count." He grinned at his wife. Shanice was a professional landscaper.

"Evan wants a puppy for Christmas," Penelope said.

"Get him one. He's at the perfect age, and dogs are wonderful companions."

"I work a lot. It isn't fair to the dog. Dogs love people."

"I'll give you the time off." Lincoln teased. "And Evan gets off many school holidays. It seems like the kids are hardly ever in school. Now in my day ..."

"Things were exactly the same. However, it's food for thought and you're both too kind." Penelope was grateful for their welcoming invitation, though it meant she would be alone if Evan spent nights at his uncle's house. And what about the days before Christmas when he was scheduled to visit his father? The visitation stipulated every other year, and this was Evan's year to visit.

The prospect tied her stomach in a knot. Christmas was such a special season, and she would be missing those precious days with her son.

How would she cope when he left for college in a few years? Kids went to college all the time, though the possibility of Evan leaving ripped at her heart.

Then she would truly be by herself.

From across the table, Lincoln grabbed her hands. "Start living your life again."

"I'm trying. It's difficult."

Her brother's advice was sound. Why did she refute him? Perhaps the best path for Evan was to allow him room to grow.

She carried her plate to the sink. "Thanks for the pie, Shanice. I'd better run. Jacob is picking me up at two o'clock."

Shanice grinned. "You're on a first-name basis with Dr. Handsome."

Penelope stood quietly for a moment before she nodded,

recognizing the meaningful smiles exchanged between her brother and Shanice. She crossed to the living room and instructed Evan to help his aunt and uncle on the farm because the tasks were endless.

He bristled before agreeing, reminding her that Uncle Lincoln had an adorable dog *and* a cat, *and* chickens, though Evan didn't have any pets.

"You own a hamster," she reminded.

He stroked the dog beside him. The cat had settled in his lap. "Christmas is coming, right? And a puppy?"

"Let's get through this semester first." Penelope planted a kiss on top of his hair.

"Say hi to Dr. Williams," Evan called out. "Tell him I'll volunteer next Saturday morning."

"I will." She stepped to the door. She planned to meet Jacob at her house because he'd insisted on driving.

She'd told Evan she was taking Jacob house-hunting, and he hadn't remarked one way or the other. She'd wondered at the time if he'd even heard her. Apparently, he had, and didn't have a problem with it.

Dr. Williams. Jacob. She was spending the afternoon with Jacob. Her stomach tightened, full of odd flutters she couldn't define.

CHAPTER 5

At exactly two o'clock, Penelope peeked out the living room window just as Jacob drove up to her house in his bright-yellow Volkswagen.

She'd changed when she'd returned home, deciding on lightweight linen slacks and her favorite flowered blouse. She left the blouse untucked to cover her generous waistline.

For the next hour, she slid in and out of Jacob's car to view different areas of Roses, and soon discovered that her slacks and blouse were completely wrinkled. Fortunately, her sneakers were comfortable.

She'd worn this same outfit behind a desk in an air-conditioned office several times in the past. Today, she'd imagined driving by a few neighborhoods with Jacob, then sitting across from him at her favorite coffee shop while sipping a vanilla latte.

He, on the other hand, was dressed more appropriately in khaki shorts and a green cotton golf shirt.

"You look gorgeous," he'd said when he arrived at her front door. She'd flushed with the compliment, though now she felt plain. Her blouse had soiled when they'd peered into the grimy window of an abandoned, dilapidated house on Brook Street. Dusty sunshine filled the interior.

"I like the house," he remarked, when they were once again settled in his car and headed back to town. "I like Victorian homes."

"You're joking," she said. "I wouldn't know where to begin except to hire a bulldozer."

"I'll grant the house is in dire need of repairs. But it has good bones."

"Bones? Let's start with the roof."

"What's wrong with the roof?"

"It's caving in," she reminded. "Are you handy with tools?"

He smirked. "I don't even own a tool kit, though I guess I should put it on my Christmas list if I buy the house. However, this location is excellent."

She surveyed the street. "There are several mom-and-pop stores in the area."

"The home is big."

"Unlike your car," she observed.

He chuckled and patted the dashboard. "Can't beat compact and reliable."

He switched on the radio to a contemporary station. She recognized the holiday tune, remarking that it wasn't even Halloween yet and they were playing Christmas music. Jacob tapped the rhythm of "It's the Most Wonderful Time of the Year" on the steering wheel and sang in a deep baritone voice.

"The house has what I want most," he continued when he'd finished singing.

"Which is?" she asked.

"Besides you?"

"Get outta here."

He grinned. "I'll tell you when we arrive in town."

Despite the outfit mistake, she enjoyed the hours with

him. He was interesting, with a grand sense of humor and a clear disdain for the other homes they drove by. He seemed to gravitate to the old, rundown house.

Finally, they took a break for cups of sweet lemonade from a sidewalk stand.

"Soon, the downtown will decorate for the holidays." Penelope gestured up and down the street. "We even hold a bake-off contest."

"We?"

"Yes. I'm a resident of the town." She admonished him with amused severity.

He grinned. "Me, too."

"Keiran and Desiree, a husband-and-wife team, own O'Malley's Irish pub. Keiran bakes whiskey cakes. He usually wins the contest because his cakes are delicious, although Desiree's pistachio cake is equally delicious."

"I've never baked so much as a cupcake, but I'll patronize a good bakery any day." Jacob chuckled. "I lived in Atlanta for many years and there are several well-known bakeries specializing in smiling gingerbread men and chocolate Santas around the holidays."

"I love sweets," she admitted with a sigh. "However, I'm set on healthy eating in order to lose a few pounds."

"I agree with the healthy eating part." Jacob swept an arm around her shoulders and gave a caring squeeze. "In Atlanta, a spectacular Stone Mountain Christmas serves all sorts of food. Some might be healthy."

"You'll love the holiday events here, too," she said. "Food trucks line the streets on weekends in December. If you're up for a thirty-minute drive, an entire town lights up every house for Christmas and is utterly charming."

"I look forward to seeing it. So far, Roses reminds me of a Rockwell painting." Jacob placed a hand on the small of

Penelope's back while directing her toward a bench. "I hope you'll accompany me to Atlanta."

Her heart thumped a joyful beat. Jacob wanted to include her in his Christmas plans.

"On one condition." Penelope balanced the cup of lemonade in her hands and situated herself on the bench. "You allow me to treat."

"Nope."

She took in a breath, about to object, and he shook his head. "I'm aware you don't date, so we won't call it a date. Like today. Today isn't a date."

"Today is a house-hunting day."

"Exactly."

Good. He'd gotten the message, though she suddenly felt empty despite her firm assertions. Apparently, her emotions hadn't gotten the same message.

No, no, no. She couldn't be falling for him. Wasn't her unsuccessful marriage, her pathetic attempts at dating, evidence enough?

"Romance is off the table for me," she declared, to firm up her assertion. "My last attempt was dating a teacher at my son's school. I wanted to like him because he was a great guy. He was fun, but we always ran out of things to talk about. I wondered after I broke it off with him if it was him or me. Either way, I wasn't willing to commit to anything beyond a shared pizza."

"No dates. No pizza." Jacob saluted her. "Romance memo received, loud and clear."

She drew a long breath and groped for a subject change. "Candee mentioned you were a discriminating house buyer. Today I witnessed firsthand what she meant."

"I'm certain she used a stronger word than discriminating."

"Her description was 'picky.'"

"Completely true." His mouth twisted in amusement. "I intend to establish a practice in my home, and my choice is important both professionally and personally."

"You're looking for a house big enough to live in *and* practice medicine?"

"Yes. A neighborhood made up of both businesses and residential." He gestured up and down the block. "Similar to your area."

"Why?" she asked.

"Homey. Convenience. I'll be more available for my patients. In Atlanta, my practice was becoming more of a business. Something happened ... several things, and I realized I needed to make a change."

She offered a murmur of acknowledgement when he didn't supply any additional information. "Why did you become a doctor?"

"As I mentioned, my family moved to the States, and because of the bankruptcy, all we could afford was a mobile home in an impoverished area. We had nothing at first, not even furniture. We'd sit on the living room floor and pray." At her quizzical expression, he explained, "Me, my mum, father, sister."

"And then?"

"And then God delivered. We worked odd jobs and eventually scraped up enough money to purchase several acres of farmland." He drained his lemonade, then gazed at her. "My mum wanted me to stay on the farm and help. In fact, she suggested I quit school early. She doesn't believe education is important."

"And?"

"I refused. When I graduated, I got out of town as soon as I could and never looked back."

"Your parents still live on the farm?"

"My mum does."

"Your father?"

"He disappeared several years ago. He's not the sort of guy who sticks around when the going gets rough."

"Who helps your mother with—" Penelope began.

"My sister lives in Maryland." He closed his eyes for a beat. "I understand my mum's concerns. After all, she's alone and running a farm. But I couldn't. I just couldn't stay, only to please her."

Penelope gazed back at him, giving him her full attention. "You're not a farmer?"

"Hardly. I can't even grow an herb."

"One can never have too many herbs."

He grinned, obviously appreciative of her attempt to ease the conversation, but soon sobered. "There were few doctors or dentists where I grew up. My sister married young, and her daughter, Linda, ... an accident occurred when she was seven."

He breathed in a deep lungful of air. His silence, a heartfelt emotion, was so palpable she could almost taste it.

"Go on. I didn't intend to ask so many questions." But yes. Yes, she did.

She waited for his reply and scanned the park across the way, the children running and playing tag. Autumn was a magnificent season. Gold and red leaves twirled to the ground, and the landscape was splashed with color.

She acknowledged several parents as they pushed their toddlers on the swings. This was the advantage of small-town living. Some called it a downside, though she understood both sides.

"Linda didn't receive the adequate care required for her condition, at least, not in my opinion," Jacob continued. "Our community lacked quality medical doctors. Soon afterwards, I decided to become a doctor and make a difference. Somewhere along the line, I got sidetracked while climbing the ladder of success. I strove to be the best in my field."

"That's a good thing."

"Maybe I wanted to prove something."

"To whom?"

He didn't reply for a moment. "Maybe my mum. Maybe myself."

"Were you the best?"

"I accepted a position at one of the country's leading children's hospitals." He opened his cell phone and scrolled to the photos, tapping a picture of a hospital sign to make it larger.

Penelope recognized the Atlanta hospital immediately. "Impressive. Congratulations."

"Thanks. I was passed over several times when I applied for the position of public health and administrative leadership. This last time was the final straw. I was experienced, and the most qualified for the job."

"So, you quit?"

"An administrative role was my biggest dream. I worked my entire career for the opportunity. I wanted more, more, more." He met her gaze. "I sound bitter, don't I?"

"A little. You're human." She tilted her head back to view him better. His recklessly handsome features regarded her. His face was captivating, almost boyish, especially when the strong jawline and keenly carved mouth were changed by one of his devastating smiles.

Beyond them, bluebirds flew through the air, spinning and diving from tree to tree. She had the urge to slip off her shoes and relish the cool grass tickling her toes.

"I'm learning how to be content and follow my focus to help people, though I may disappoint others," he said. "Life is an interesting balance."

"Balance between what?"

"Contentment and complacency. I never want to be complacent."

"Like me?"

"You're not complacent."

"I haven't changed jobs yet," she reminded him.

"Your job is important." He tucked his cell phone back in his pocket. "Just remember not to limit yourself."

"The family business is what I know."

"All my life, I questioned my career choices and long hours," he said. "I couldn't put my finger on what needed to change. When I quit my job in Atlanta, I visited several areas in search of a medical practice to purchase. Then I learned Dr. Damian's office was available, and here I am. It's odd how things work out. I never considered a small town setting before ..."

"Because a small town is beneath your big city aspirations?"

"Thanks, Penelope."

"The salary and benefits are obviously greater in Atlanta."

"No question. My job was becoming soulless, though."

"Do you ... intend on settling here permanently?"

"Yes." He regarded her. His expression changed, turning thoughtful. He rubbed his thumb along her palm and raised her hand to his lips.

Her heart lurched. "Why Roses?"

"Hard-working, down-to-earth folks are the best." Lightly, he kissed her fingers, and her hand tingled. "I'm a medical man and serving in a large hospital was rewarding for two decades, but circumstances led to my change of heart, and the end result is a blessing."

Her eyes widened as she digested his remark. "What circumstances?"

"What do you mean?"

"Circumstances suggest more than one thing happened."

She slid her hand away and tucked it securely behind her back. "You mentioned being passed over for the higher hospital positions. What was the other circumstance?"

"Sad, sad story." He suddenly became absorbed with studying the brick pavement. "A family tragedy."

"Your niece?"

He didn't reply.

"Your mother?"

"She's okay. We only talk when I reach out to her."

Penelope set her cup down and touched his forearm. Whatever the tragedy, he preferred to keep the heartache to himself.

"I'm glad you chose to land in Roses," she finally said.

"Me too." His intense brown eyes locked with hers, and a quiver of attraction shot through her.

"Lucky you."

"Why?"

"You heard all my problems on the plane." A thought occurred. "I'm surprised I didn't scare you off."

"If anything, I was more intrigued." He pointed to a simple, wood-sided building. "Look. Roses has an animal shelter."

"I'm well aware. Evan reminds me every day on the way to school when we pass by."

"Have you ever stopped in?"

She nodded. "We've visited several times. The precious animals break my heart and I want to bring all of them home. Almost two months ago, the shelter took in a pregnant stray. They think she is a terrier mix, mostly Scottish."

"How soon is she due?"

"She had her puppies."

"An entire litter for Christmas?" He tried to suppress a smile. "Evan will be thrilled. How many?"

"On average, dogs have five to ten puppies. She had six." Penelope swallowed a bubble of laughter. "Good try, Jacob."

"All that pleasure in one litter and you're still deciding? Psst. Cats are easier." Playfully, he nudged her. "Let's go see for ourselves."

Penelope picked up their cups and discarded them in the trash. A few minutes later, they climbed the stairs and walked through the shelter's doors.

"Be forewarned," a volunteer teasingly wagged her finger. "You'll probably fall in love."

"I'm inquiring about the terrier mix," Penelope said. "She recently had puppies."

The volunteer bobbed her head. "The dog is out back. The vet is examining her. Are you ready to bring a sweet furry friend home today? She is on our VIP status."

"Meaning?" Jacob asked.

"She's been here a while, and we don't want her to be overlooked." The volunteer met Jacob's gaze.

"I'm interested in possibly adopting one of her puppies," Penelope said.

She and Jacob peered into the cages as they walked down the aisles. Dogs with expressive, adoring eyes stared back at them. Penelope wanted to pass her fingers through the soft fur of each dog—colors of apricot, gray, silver, brown and black. Whether the dog's characteristics resembled a pug or a husky, they all had the cutest faces.

The volunteer announced that the mother dog, named Nutcracker, had been brought back to her cage, and they all stepped over. The dog's compact build and short legs, distinctive white coat and overall sturdiness, brought a heartfelt smile to Penelope's lips.

"This dog is more precious every time I see her," she said.

"I agree. She is gorgeous." He glanced at the volunteer. "May I pet her?"

The volunteer opened the cage and the dog stepped out. "Sure. Nutcracker will sniff you until she approves."

"Right." Jacob bent down and held his hand in a fist. He averted his gaze so that he wasn't looking directly at the dog. Once he passed the sniff test, he gently petted the dog's shoulders.

Penelope crouched down with him and smiled. "You're comfortable with dogs," she said.

Nutcracker, apparently satisfied, turned and found a cozy spot in her cage.

Six squirming, wriggling puppies with pink markings on their tiny paws, playfully romped and wagged their tails. Though wobbly on their feet, their liveliness knew no bounds. All the puppies had white fur, their coats velvety and fluffy. They yipped and yelped, boisterous, and paying no attention to Penelope and Jacob.

"Two boys and four girls," the volunteer declared. She warned the puppies weren't old enough to be picked up and handled yet, as they were only approaching four weeks. Furthermore, the puppies weren't adoptable before seven to nine weeks of age.

"Which puppy are you choosing for Evan?" Jacob asked, after he thanked the volunteer. He clasped Penelope's hand and they walked back to their bench across the street.

"When the time comes, the decision will be up to him. A puppy is a huge commitment, and I'm still not certain whether Evan is up to the task," Penelope sighed. "Or if I am because I'll probably assume the brunt of the work. I'm still weighing the pros and cons."

"Tough to do."

"Depends on which side of the fence you're on. Practical, like me, or more laid-back and irresponsible, like Evan."

"I try to agree with the parent, except in this instance."

Jacob studied her for a long moment. "A puppy will teach Evan responsibility."

"You're a big help. Then I'll have a puppy and a hamster running around the house. Or six puppies, if you have your way. Please don't encourage Evan when he's at your clinic."

"I wouldn't dream of it." Jacob chuckled. "Though there's something about puppies that triggers empathy." He rested his arm along the back of the bench and turned to her, his gaze focusing on her lips.

"I can't discuss my puppy dilemma when you stare at me." She dabbed at her chin with her forefinger. "Am I dripping lemonade peel?"

He leaned toward her and rubbed his fingers along her chin. "Penelope Reid. You are lovely and I can't stop looking at you. You've successfully diverted my attention away from the puppies."

"I'm not doing anything except sitting next to you."

"Reason enough to break my concentration."

"Quit joking." She jabbed at him with her elbow.

She tried, though she couldn't tamp down the bewildering yet indisputable flurries in her chest. She felt like a teen again, all nervous and agitated and captivated by a guy.

Oh, no, she firmly reminded herself. She didn't intend to date any man, and besides, Jacob wasn't interested in her. He intended to keep things simple, if that was the correct word he used, plus he was committed to his career.

However, her impractical brain shoved the thoughts to the side.

His gaze ran along her face. "Gorgeous," he murmured, giving her an admiring smile.

She heard herself inhale but didn't move.

He bent his head. Softly, he kissed her, his lips touching hers. "You taste so sweet," he whispered.

"Lemons are sour," she teased.

"But lemonade is sweet."

"We can't begin anything, Jacob. I'm not looking for a relationship."

"Neither am I."

At least he was honest, although for some reason, his admission disappointed her. She covered her disappointment with a topic switch. "Roses needed an excellent pediatrician and all-round doctor. The residents are thrilled you're here."

"All the residents?"

"Every single one."

"Good." His lips were still close, his gaze hooded. Evidently, he wasn't self-conscious about kissing her in the middle of town. His scent was clean—the outdoors coupled with a trace of male. She pushed down the urge to wrap her arms around him, to feel the hard muscles of his forearms, his cotton shirt pressed against her cheek.

"I plan to serve the community, then I will ease up to pursue things I enjoy," he murmured. "I hope you'll do the same."

If he referred to her wooden dolls, she'd moved the craft to a back burner. "Things like what?"

"Things like—" His eyebrows drew together as his cell phone pinged. He read the message and stood. "I'm sorry, Penelope, but we'll have to forego our dinner plans for another evening. An emergency has come up at the clinic."

She stood alongside him. "Nothing serious, I hope?"

"A preteen girl swallowed a bee." He typed a response into his phone. "I recommended to the head nurse that the girl drink water, but I'll see her just in case."

"Will she be okay?"

"I look for localized swelling, though she may suffer mild pain."

Penelope matched his long strides to the car. Several times, his hands brushed against hers. When he parked at the curb of her home a few minutes later, he cracked the windows open, letting in a breeze, and apologized again.

"Such is the life of a pediatrician. I'll double my efforts to wow you by treating you to the fanciest place in town. There is an exquisite farm to table restaurant getting rave reviews." He flashed a grin before dashing around to the passenger side to open the door for her. He'd opened the door when he'd picked her up earlier, too. He was a polite, considerate man. She liked that about him.

"Please, Jacob, don't apologize, and a fancy dinner isn't required."

"It's not a date, Penelope," he said. "We'll call our time together something else."

"Like what?"

He kissed her temple, then whispered in her ear, "I'll think of something."

CHAPTER 6

*S*unday mornings meant church, and this Sunday was no exception. As always, Penelope and Evan attended the eleven o'clock service. The church hadn't begun to decorate for the holidays yet, though a live nativity was planned for December.

Penelope chose a long-sleeved jersey-knit dress in sage green and topped the dress with a shawl-collared coat in a light khaki. She wore her hair loose, and when she peered at herself in the mirror, her smile was bright. She looked forward to her upcoming "undate" with Jacob.

After church, she and Evan opted for lunch at Kathleen's Tea Shop, a popular eatery.

Kathleen, the owner, had decked out her restaurant in Thanksgiving finery. Autumn-scented candles, miniature pumpkins and oranges, and golden-colored napkins created an inviting ambiance. Kathleen and her husband, Rob, were hands-on restauranteurs, and the nod was always there as a tribute to Kathleen's Irish heritage. The shamrock-green walls lent a festive flair.

As Penelope and Evan entered, the scent of yeast rolls and

fresh-brewed coffee filled the air. An Irish tenor's voice crooned a holiday tune, accompanied by a harp and fiddle.

"November is too early for Christmas music," Evan said.

"It's never too early." Penelope hummed the melody of "Holly, Jolly Christmas" along with the Irish tenor. "November is the magic time between Thanksgiving and Christmas. You can sense the spirit of anticipation. It's almost palpable."

After they were ushered to their table and seated, Evan pulled out his cell phone.

"No cell phones at the table," Penelope reminded.

With an exaggerated sigh, he tucked away the phone, perused the menu and selected pancakes, scrambled eggs, and orange juice.

"Hey, there's Dr. Williams sitting all by himself." He indicated a corner table. "Let's invite him over."

Penelope's heart skipped a beat. "I'm going out to dinner with him tonight," she replied.

"He told me when I volunteered at the clinic yesterday." Evan smiled. "He seemed excited. You do, too."

"I do?"

"Yeah. You're fun when you smile and hum Christmas songs."

She drew a quick breath. Evan was obviously more astute than she gave him credit for.

"His clinic is short-staffed," Evan said. "He wondered if you'd volunteer there in your spare time."

"He did? What spare time?"

Several days had passed since Penelope had last seen Jacob and life had marched on. He texted often, quick texts when she least expected, apologizing for his busyness. Sometimes he texted in the early morning, and she was surprised she was on his mind in the hours before dawn.

He usually began his texts with a question.

Are you awake?

Unfortunately, yes, she replied. *I hardly ever sleep.*

Same here. Once I secure more staff, I'll ease up on the hours.

Work overload. Remember why you moved here?

To help people, he typed.

From the talk in town, you've reached your goal and I'm impressed, she said. *You're an overachiever.*

How would you feel if I told you I moved here because of you?

If she were honest with herself, his question brought dreams. Dreams of a relationship. She dismissed the consideration as quickly as it surfaced. She wouldn't risk having her heart broken again.

Knock it off, she replied.

I'm looking forward to seeing you soon for our ... undate.

Is that your new favorite word?

Definitely. BTW, how is your creativity level these days?

Nonexistent.

Evan brought some of your wooden dolls to the clinic. The kids love them.

I haven't had any time for more woodcarving.

Make the time, he said.

Whenever her mind focused on him, which was often, she was touched and impressed by his story. He'd left a successful career behind to relocate to a postage-stamp community and lend a helping hand with his physician skills. In all honesty, she'd been a bit envious that he'd decided to go after what he wanted. Why couldn't she be more like him?

You're gifted, he added.

Gifted? Hardly, though she knew her cheeks flushed at his compliment.

Not easy while balancing a full-time job and raising a preteen. She stared at the phone screen. *Are you doing any more house-hunting?*

I'm fixated on the dilapidated house on Brook Street.

Why?

It's big and cheap and in an excellent location.

She sent a thinking face emoji. *Better buy that tool kit. You'll need it.*

LOL. I haven't had a chance to drive by recently. Should I make an offer? I'm pondering pros and cons and all that. Thanks again for the tour of the town.

I'm happy to assist, she said.

Truth?

Always.

The other day, I was more fixated on you than on the houses.

"How do I answer him?" she muttered to the empty room. How could she tell him *she'd* been fixated on him? Think quickly, Penelope. Start a new topic.

You seem the type of person who is quick and decisive, she typed.

Truth?

Again?

I'm decisive at work. In my personal life, not so much.

A few hours later, Jacob texted:

Good news. I've secured extra help at the clinic. I'm free on Sunday night.

For more house-hunting?

For dinner at the farm to table restaurant. Will you join me?

Somehow, he'd avoided the word date.

Sure.

See you soon, beautiful.

Please, Jacob, don't flatter me.

Why not?

I'm unaccustomed to compliments.

Get accustomed ... you are beautiful.

A smile overtook her face when she bid him a good night. He always closed his texts by calling her beautiful. He made it clear he found her attractive, and he boosted her self-esteem. She recalled the numerous instances when her father, or her ex, had muttered slighting comments about her weight. They were hurtful and hadn't helped in her effort to lead a healthier lifestyle.

She smiled. Seeing Jacob at the restaurant and thinking of his texts brought a flip of excitement she could hardly hide.

"Mom?" Evan craned his neck and waved at Jacob. "Can Dr. Williams join us?"

"Sure."

Evan jumped to his feet and hurried toward Jacob's table.

She closed the menu, deciding on coffee and toast, then looked around at the beaming couples and chatting relatives. She did love this little town. Life was slower, summer and fall had waned, and November brought a decided crispness to the air. Nearby, a toddler chortled with laughter as her father tickled her and the young mother smiled in approval.

Such a precious family, Penelope mused. Christmas will be extra special for them.

She'd always wanted more than one baby and envisioned celebrating noisy, over-the-top Christmases, but her dreaded birthday loomed, and her child-bearing years were over. The only child she had to hang onto was Evan.

She set aside her contemplations and gave her attention to Evan as he advanced with Jacob in tow. Jacob paused at a couple near them, apparently recognizing their child. He conversed with the parents and squatted beside the boy. With a broad smile, he playfully interacted, and the boy's dimples flashed. Jacob seemed genuinely interested and concerned, lingering, and chatting. He was excellent with children.

He wore navy-blue pants and a checkered button-up shirt. Again, she was struck by his athletic physique and confident manner. When he approached, he greeted her with a twinkle in his deep-brown eyes.

Sometimes, though, she detected sadness in those same eyes.

With an undisputable flutter of magnetism, she greeted him. "Hi, Jacob. Please have a seat."

"Thanks." He claimed a chair between her and Evan. "I heard a lot about this place and wanted to check it out after church this morning."

"We were at church, too. I didn't see you."

"I sat in the back."

"We sit in the front."

"Fortunately, we ended up in the same restaurant."

She lifted a brow. "What a coincidence."

He grinned. "Definitely."

He distributed the coffees and orange juice that the waitress placed on their table. "Are we still on for tonight?"

"Uh-huh."

"Two undates in one day."

Evan gulped down his orange juice. "What's an undate?"

"Private joke, mate," Jacob replied.

He poured cream into his coffee. Penelope did the same and added sugar.

"We can take a raincheck," she said.

"I wouldn't dream of it." Jacob's eyebrows furrowed, silently telling her no excuses were allowed. "I moved schedules for this evening. Sickness doesn't stop on Sundays and the clinic is well staffed. They'll do fine without me."

They placed their orders, and the waitress returned shortly and set plates of eggs, pancakes, and melted toasties on the table. A toastie was an Irish specialty sandwich, featuring cheddar cheese, ham, and onion. Complimentary Irish soda bread was also provided.

Penelope bowed her head to say grace, and Jacob and Evan followed suit.

As soon as she finished her prayer, Evan poured a gallon

of syrup on his pancakes and dove into them. When he was done, he gave her a rueful glance. "Did Dr. Williams tell you that when you finally give me permission to get a puppy, he'll go with us to the shelter to help us choose?"

"No, he never told me that."

Jacob shrugged. "I meant to."

"Dr. Williams also reminded me that Candee and Teddy Winchester raise beagle puppies." Evan finished the rest of his orange juice in one gulp. "Did you know that, Mom?"

She sighed. "I did, indeed." In a moment of weakness, she'd phoned Candee to inquire if any of her pups were available. Candee had replied that she and her husband were concentrating on their son's horses and hadn't had any time to devote to breeding or raising any more puppies.

AFTER THEIR PLATES WERE CLEARED, Evan asked to be excused and walk home.

"The tea shop is quite far from home," Penelope protested.

"Don't freak out, Mom. You encouraged me to get more exercise."

She eyed her son. Despite church that morning, he'd insisted on wearing his usual baggy jeans and an oversized T-shirt of a band she'd never heard of. Once, he'd prided himself on clean, stylish clothes, which she'd deemed remarkable for a young boy. Sometime this past year, she'd couldn't pinpoint exactly when, he'd stopped being concerned about his appearance.

Now, as he slumped back in his chair, he didn't seem surly or rebellious. He just seemed reconciled to the fact that there was no use in arguing with her.

Jacob pushed his coffee cup to the side. "How about if he walks to my clinic instead? Only a few blocks from here and two nurses are working this afternoon." He waved his cell phone in the air. "I'm on call, as usual."

Evan met Jacob's explanation with a bland expression. "Will I have to work?"

"I expect you'll make yourself useful," Jacob said. "Zack is volunteering today. You can carry out a list of phone calls together."

Evan's eyes narrowed. "You just gave me a good reason not to go."

"Why would you say such a thing?" Penelope folded her hands in her lap. "Zack is your friend."

Evan stared at the floor. "You wouldn't understand."

"Try me."

"I'm a joke to the other kids, Mom, remember? They tease me all the time."

"Treat your mum with respect, mate," Jacob said. "She asked you a question."

"Sorry, Mom."

"The other kids tease you?" Penelope leaned forward. "Even Zack?"

"Not him so much. But some of the boys at my school push me around."

A flicker of alarm added to the despair creeping up her chest. Evan was too young to defend himself. Why hadn't he confided in her? No child should be harassed, and she had a good mind to phone Zack's mother.

She brushed his arm. "Are you telling me—"

Evan flinched at her touch. His ears burned a bright red. "I don't want to talk about it anymore, okay?"

"You were bullied at school?" Penelope demanded. "When?"

"In the boy's locker room after gym practice. One of the guys pushed past me so hard I fell on the floor."

"Why didn't you tell me any of this before?"

His gaze lowered. "I'm telling you now, Mom."

Jacob regarded Evan with a quiet expression. They fastened eyes before Evan fixated his gaze on the window.

"Did Zack see any of this?" she asked.

"He was in the locker room." Evan refused to meet her gaze. "When I fell, the other kids laughed, but Zack just walked away."

"He should've defended you. You two are friends."

"Yeah, like when we were ten."

Penelope placed a hand on Evan's arm again. "I'll call the school and complain."

"Are you kidding? Everyone hates me. Let me quit and we can live on Uncle Lincoln's houseboat forever." He swiped at his eyes and shoved back his chair. "May I leave now?"

"Where are you going?" Penelope pulled her cell phone from her purse.

"I'll go to the clinic and ignore Zack."

"How will you get home? Do you want me to pick you up?"

"I'll drive him," Jacob put in.

"Thanks." Evan turned to Jacob. "I'll finish phoning more hospitals for supplies, right, Dr. Williams?"

"You're a born salesman." Jacob trapped Penelope's wrist. "Who are you calling?" he quietly asked as they watched her son leave the restaurant.

She shook off his hand and scrolled through her phone. "I might have Zack's number in my contacts. I'll talk to his mother."

"Don't." He caught her gaze and held it. "The more you try to mediate the situation, the worse his friendships and school will be. Let him and Zack work it out for themselves."

"Are you an authority on children now?"

"Kids can be cruel." He broke eye contact, his conviction flat and firm.

"Evan is an innocent child. He doesn't deserve to be picked on."

"No one does." Jacob lowered his voice. His expression was strained. "I grew up dirt-poor. I didn't wear the right clothes. I talked funny because of my Aussie accent, and not a day went by that I wasn't teased or bullied."

"You couldn't help your family's situation."

"True."

"I still feel sad for Evan."

"He'll be okay." His cell phone buzzed with an incoming text. He read the text. His dark eyebrows furrowed as he pushed back his chair. "I need to head to the hospital."

"An accident?"

"A woman was washing a glass in the sink and the glass broke. She needs stitches in her hand."

"Dr. Williams?" A striking, well-groomed woman in a figure-hugging red pantsuit, a woman Penelope recognized from Evan's school, stopped at their table. "I'm Meredith Sinclair. Do you remember me?"

Jacob inclined his head. "Of course."

"I assume I'm not interrupting anything." She flipped back her shiny blond hair and granted Penelope a quick scan. "Do you two know each other?"

"We're best friends and tell each other our deepest, darkest secrets." Jacob smiled at Penelope. His joking tone conveyed a note of fun, though his gaze was serious.

Penelope was ready to refute him, but he grabbed her hand across the table and squeezed. "Right, mate?"

His amused expression irked her. "You wish, mate," she refuted sarcastically.

Meredith cut her eyes to Penelope, then back to Jacob. "I wanted to personally thank you, Dr. Williams. My daughter, Annabelle, recovered quickly from the bee incident."

"I'm glad. How is she feeling?"

"Your quick thinking made all the difference." She gave him a flirtatious smile. "I'm speaking for the entire community when I say we're thrilled you set up a practice here in Roses."

He paused, seeming to reflect on her words. "My pleasure. Annabelle is a lovely girl."

"Thank you." Meredith turned to Penelope, finally taking more than a passing interest. "All the mothers in Annabelle's class are having a Christmas cookie exchange next month at my house. Would you like to join us? I know Evan is in her homeroom."

"If I'm free, I'll try to be there," Penelope said. "Please send me the details."

"Annabelle will give Evan the information."

Meredith Sinclair had never been one of Penelope's favorite parents. The man she'd recently divorced was a flagrant attorney, and the family had a high-class air not lost on Penelope. From what she recalled, Annabelle was pretty and popular in school.

Once she swished away, Penelope remarked, "The girl who swallowed the bee was Annabelle?"

"Yup. Do you know the family?"

"A little, though Meredith snubbed me, as usual," Penelope said. "Our kids have been in the same classes ever since I moved back here."

"She didn't snub you. She invited you to a cookie exchange."

Penelope fumbled, dumbfounded that Jacob stuck up for Meredith. She checked her watch. "Evan should be arriving at your clinic by now."

"He'll see Zack," Jacob reminded. He picked up the check. Despite her objection, he firmly shook his head and placed several bills, plus a generous tip, on the table. "I'll stop at the clinic after I finish at the hospital."

"Let me know if he and Zack talk at all."

"Please, Penelope, allow him some freedom." Jacob bent down and kissed the top of her head before she could turn away.

She stiffened.

"Is anything wrong?" he asked.

"Of course not." She'd heard a sermon once about being a stuffer and keeping her emotions inside, instead of letting them out. She'd honed that skill to a tee.

"Remember," his puzzled smile confronted her, "I know everything about you."

"Almost everything," she corrected.

"You can't hide your emotions from me."

"Try me."

"I'll pick you up at seven o'clock tonight for our undate."

"Where are we going? The farm to table restaurant?"

"Nope Dress casual." He gave a lopsided grin. "The location is a surprise."

CHAPTER 7

$\mathcal{I}$t was a surprise all right, because the "undate" never occurred.

Jacob phoned an hour after Penelope arrived home. She'd changed into a red sweatshirt, as a nod to the upcoming holidays, and black sweatpants for comfort. Now she stood in the kitchen and clicked her cell phone on speaker as she pulled a tray of cream cheese Christmas cookies from the oven. The recipe had been handed down from her great-grandmother, Teresa, and she baked a double batch every year, mindful to send a plate to the first responders in town. Later in the season, she'd hand-deliver a batch to the local police station, too.

"I can't apologize enough," Jacob began. "Unfortunately, I need to cancel tonight."

She lowered her head and pressed her lips tight. "Another emergency?"

"A head injury. A ten-year-old child fell off his bike and is experiencing confusion. The parents are beyond worried and a little crazy."

Sternly, she reminded herself that her disappointment stemmed from selfishness.

He'd committed himself to serving people, and his kind and concerned attitude showed. He had so many good traits, which made her care for him even more.

She tossed a dishtowel over her shoulder. "Are the parents overreacting?"

"They're sensitive, though I tried to explain the situation. The child is being transferred to the hospital to be monitored overnight. Once I finish at the clinic, I'll stop by the hospital to check on him."

She placed the tray on top of the stove. "Your patients come first."

"I appreciate your understanding. I didn't anticipate a nurse calling in sick or a child's worrisome head injury."

Juggling the difficult emergencies a pediatrician dealt with daily was difficult to imagine. He never complained. He strove for a work-life balance, though parents were emotional and easily upset when it came to the well-being of their children.

"I'll make it up to you," he said.

"Don't be ridiculous."

"Do you like flowers?"

"Everyone likes flowers."

"What's your favorite?"

"No one has asked me the question before because …"

"Don't stop now."

"Because no one ever brought me flowers." She struggled between maintaining her self-respect and answering truthfully. An irrefutable pang of sadness twisted her gut.

"You haven't answered my question."

"Roses. I love red roses."

He chuckled. "Befitting, considering the town we live in."

She grabbed a cookie off the tray and bit into it. Mmm.

Delicious. She swung her arms as she made her way to the sink. Food always cheered her up.

"I'm baking Christmas cookies," she said.

"For Meredith Sinclair's cookie exchange?"

"Possibly." She bristled at the woman's name, a wave of unfounded jealousy causing her to pause. "In any event, I'll freeze the cookies for now."

"I'd be tempted to cheat and pull them out of the freezer. There wouldn't be any left by Christmas."

Slightly pacified, she laughed. "Last year, I ate a half gallon of ice cream along with the cookies I had baked," she admitted.

She flicked a glance out the kitchen bay window framing her sizable backyard. The pergola-covered patio was brick paved and the table and chairs carved from teak wood. She and Evan hardly used the outdoor space. Though she paid a landscaper to mow the lawn, the curved flower bed in the corner was sorely neglected.

In fact, her entire house was untidy.

She vacillated. Should she sit beneath the pergola devouring a tray of cookies while feeling sorry for herself because of the change of plans with Jacob, or work on her housekeeping skills?

Dappled sunshine shone through the trees, and the sun began to set.

A sudden worried thought made her stomach clench. "Is Evan at the clinic?"

"He phoned several hospitals for equipment we might be able to use, then went off with Zack and his mother to the rec center."

She wasn't certain if Jacob was teasing or serious.

Evan left the clinic without phoning her?

"Oh?" Her voice swelled.

"Oh?"

The stillness between their connection troubled her. She expected a quick, clear response and shook her head in disapproval.

"Evan didn't call or text me?" She cupped the phone to her ear and paced the kitchen. Her tone was accusatory, but she couldn't help herself.

"Does he need to ask your permission first?"

"He was supposed to ride home with you."

"I told you I'm working late. There was a change of plans."

"Without informing me? His mother?" Conflicted thoughts swept through her. She'd anticipated seeing Jacob. More importantly, her son was in a car with someone else and hadn't consulted her.

"Zack's mother is a responsible adult," Jacob continued.

Restless, she shifted and didn't immediately respond. Jacob was a pediatrician, not a parent. Therefore, he wouldn't understand.

"Is Evan headed home after the rec center?" she asked.

"I assume so," Jacob said.

"That's it? No concern?"

"Look, Penelope, let me share something with you. I overheard the two boys talking about the locker room incident. It sounded like Evan shoved the boy first. Then the boy pushed him back and Evan landed on the floor."

She slumped in a chair. "I believe my son's side of the story."

"There are usually two sides to every story."

"What should I do?"

"Be aware of the situation. Junior high is challenging for most preteens, and Evan faces a bigger hurdle because he lacks a father figure."

She bristled. Jacob made it sound like Evan's home environment was lacking, though she didn't have a choice. Roy had cheated on her. As a single parent, she strove to raise her son properly and conscientiously. However, some part of her acknowledged that Jacob's words were true. An involved, interested father figure in Evan's life might make a difference, and Roy lived too far away for more than an occasional visit. Maneuvering the tricky landscape of adolescence required Evan to sort difficult decisions, and a male brought different parenting qualities than a female. Could a man bring extra value to Evan's development?

Her job as a mother was to protect her son. After all, Evan was her only family. They were a team.

"Evan and Zack spoke at length," Jacob said. "They installed a new diving board at the pool and Zack wanted to show it to Evan. Zack's mother said it wouldn't be for long."

"Okay."

"Penelope?"

"Yes?"

"Evan won't live in a bubble forever and you can't fight every battle for him. Young people solve problems without our interference all the time and turn out just fine."

She massaged her temple with both hands. "So, you're saying I should force him to man up and tough it out?"

"No one's forcing Evan to do anything."

Isn't that exactly what you're inferring? she inwardly refuted. Jacob's statements were absurd, though she told herself not to be rude and argue with him.

Offering a stiff goodbye, she clicked off the phone, arranged the cookies on a plate, and set them on the kitchen table.

She plopped on a chair and perched her chin on her hands.

She didn't like the idea of Jacob interfering in her

parenting decisions, especially when he disagreed with her, or his judgmental inference. Surely, he meant well, but she was decidedly sensitive regarding anything to do with Evan.

In what had begun as an encouraging Sunday, discouragement washed over her. She'd looked forward to the evening with Jacob more than she'd recognized. She liked the idea of a surprise dinner. She liked the romantic idea of an "undate." And she might not like to admit it, but she was sorely disheartened she wouldn't be seeing him.

Oh, no. I'll not be getting involved in a relationship that only leads to heartache.

Jacob, whether he realized it or not, had upset her with his parenting inference.

After a deep breath, she peered at the unwashed dishes and cookie sheets cluttering the sink. The floor needed sweeping. But how could she accomplish any tasks when she lacked the drive and motivation to overcome her frustration?

She sunk deeper into her thoughts, and only one emerged.

Jacob.

Feeling emotions she could hardly rationalize, she was caring for him more and more despite their differences.

He was an earnest person. His appealing smile, his charming accent, his gentlemanly mannerisms—were all qualities she longed for in a man. He was indisputably interested in Evan and wanted to build a rapport with him. Securing a bond between them seemed important to him.

She'd tried to act like it wasn't any big deal Jacob had moved to town, but even her son had noted she smiled more often, and her brother inquired if she had spent a recent afternoon soaking up the sun because of the rosy color in her cheeks. Shanice joked that Penelope must be drinking an abundance of wine for dinner.

Though now, the reality of her life threatened to consume her.

Jacob couldn't be counted on. Her son would be leaving soon to see his father. All that added up to loneliness at the holidays. Again.

She eyed the cookies on the table and pushed the plate away. She wasn't hungry anymore.

Sure, she could stuff herself with cookies ... or ... she could be more like Jacob. He'd pressed aside his former ambitions and was pursuing a lifestyle change. He'd determined what he wanted and was going after it.

Why couldn't she be as brave?

Filled with renewed energy, she refused to brood. Instead, she'd harness her disappointment and grow.

She placed the cookies in a freezer bag and stashed them in the back of the freezer.

A scan down the hallway was a stark reminder of her untidiness. She was never the neatest person, but she wasn't a slob, either.

She peered down at her outfit. Sweatshirt and sweatpants. Before her divorce, she'd dressed stylish and sophisticated.

She fixed her hands on her hips and studied herself in the mirror over the stove. "It's time," she declared, "to begin an overhaul Penelope project."

She began with her upstairs closet and spent time organizing and tossing handfuls of drab, plain clothes into bags to donate to Goodwill. The next hour she straightened the house.

While she waited for Evan to return, she wandered to the living room and grabbed a book she'd purchased about changing careers. She sat on the plush couch and penciled in her preferences, first and foremost creating toy dolls out of wood, though she found herself writing Jacob's name on the corner pages.

Her next book choice was a romance novel she'd read several times. A woman could read these books over and over, she decided. She skimmed her favorite emotional scenes and closed the book with a happy sigh.

She glanced at her watch. Hmm. Evan still wasn't home. Should she text him?

No. She'd heed Jacob's advice and wait.

She selected another book on the coffee table she'd recently purchased: *Change Your Holiday Menu, Change Your Life.* She curled up on the couch perusing healthy, nutritious meals.

Career choices, cleaning, and cooking were all steps to confront her concerns and get a handle on poor eating habits. Inspired, she marched into the kitchen and chose fresh spinach and a bag of potatoes from the pantry.

Thirty minutes later, Evan still hadn't arrived. Surely, the center was closed by now. Her concerned thoughts were interrupted by her ringing cell phone.

Her heart jumped.

"Penelope?"

She bit down on her bottom lip. "Yes?"

"This is Zack's mother. We stopped at the rec center after the clinic."

Penelope could hardly focus. "I'm aware."

"Well, we were in an accident."

"Is everyone okay?" The terror in Penelope's throat altered her breathing. She could hardly catch her breath. "Is Evan hurt?"

"We're all fine. Evan will explain. I'm dropping him off at your house shortly."

. . .

WHEN A PINK-CHEEKED Evan arrived home a few minutes later, he greeted Penelope with a smile.

"Zack's mother phoned. Thank goodness you're all right." Penelope lunged to hug him. He seemed to tolerate her for several seconds, then moved away.

"Tell me you're okay," she said.

"I'm okay, Mom."

She flopped on a chair. "What happened?"

"Zack's mother drove into a mailbox when she was making a U-turn near the rec center."

"She should've called me sooner."

"No reason to. In a few years, I'll be driving."

"We'll see about that."

"In our state, I can drive as soon as I'm sixteen."

She held her tongue and refused to comment.

Evan had processed her divorce from his father with stoic naivety and seemed to grasp that his world would never be the same. Friends had commended his strength, and Penelope was grateful to her brother and the toy shop. They'd given her a solid purpose to return to Roses and piece her life together.

With a pang of guilt, she recognized her own strict childhood, coupled with the realization that life was tenuous, might be the reasons she was holding her son back.

With a quiet exhale, she knew there were few powers more potent than a strongminded, soon-to-be adolescent.

"Dr. Williams called to let me know where you were." She stood, telling herself not to dwell on the accident. She tossed the spinach into a salad with boiled eggs and a light vinaigrette dressing. "So, how was your afternoon with Zack?"

"It wasn't as bad as I thought." Evan placed his jacket on a chair. "You'd be surprised at the rec center's transformation. The entire place has been remodeled."

"I'd like to see it some time." She set the salad and potatoes on the table. "I haven't been there in over a year. Not since you quit swimming."

He didn't react, though he stepped farther into the kitchen and surveyed the food. "Looks good, Mom."

"Thanks. Did you guys go anywhere after the rec center?"

His face blanched. "We stayed for a while, stopped for hamburgers and milk shakes, and then Zack's mother ran into the mailbox."

You're lying, she thought. But about what? She decided not to pry and gestured to the table. "I roasted potatoes, too."

"Yeah. I'd prefer chips, though."

She grabbed the cookbook. "I'm trying out new recipes for Christmas Day."

"I'll be home by then. Don't we usually eat lasagna?"

"Different foods make life interesting, Evan." She cocked her head to the side to take in the sight of her sweet son. "I'll miss you while you're visiting your father."

"You'll only be alone a few days."

"Your father said that baby Christina weighed eight pounds and eleven ounces when she was born." Penelope's voice quavered. "Childhood is so precious. Remember when I used to read the Christmas story to you on Christmas day?"

Evan went to the sink to wash his hands, then turned to search her face. She forced a smile, although he obviously noted the sadness in her expression.

"You can read the story to me again, Mom. I like it. In the meantime, visit with Uncle Lincoln and Aunt Shanice if you miss me."

"They're flying to New York City on an extended holiday." She flipped through the pages of the cookbook and came across a recipe featuring quinoa and bell peppers. She held it up for him to see. "I'm still concerned about you flying all by yourself."

"I'm finally twelve," Evan said. "It's legal for me to fly without an adult."

"I'm still not comfortable with the idea." She flopped down on a chair. It seemed as if she was more protective of him than ever.

"What about Dr. Williams?" Evan sank into the chair across from her, whispered a prayer of grace, and scarfed down a baked potato. "You can hang out with him at the clinic. When I come back on Christmas Eve day, we'll invite him over. I bet he doesn't want to be alone, either."

"We'll see." She regarded the spinach salad. "Try some."

"Later." He eyed the salad and stood. "Aren't you and Dr. Williams going out to dinner tonight? That's why you're not eating, right?"

"He canceled. An emergency after you left."

Evan placed his dish in the sink. "What are you going to do instead?"

She had a mountain of office work to tackle. However, the living room screamed for a dusting.

An idea occurred. There was something else. Something to distract her. Something that never failed to trigger happy, nostalgic memories.

"Evan?"

"Hmm?" One foot in the hallway, he swiveled toward her.

"Let's lug our Christmas tree down from the attic."

"Mom, it's November. We always wait until after your birthday before we trim the house. Last year, we hardly decorated."

"Decorating is a lot of work," she reminded. She'd decided there wasn't much to celebrate once her family had split up.

She reined in her previous emotions. Was her resentment toward her ex-husband hurting her son? She shouldn't be going through the motions of Christmas. She should be truly appreciating the holiday.

"Lots of families decorate early." She hauled in a decisive breath. "This year, let's be one of those families."

AN HOUR LATER, Penelope eyed the living room with satisfaction. Sparkling white lights twinkled from the dark-green artificial spruce. Garland, in earthy tones and decorated with pinecones, dangled from the tree branches. On her front door, she hung a cedar faux wreath adorned with red berries and gold metallic bulbs, then tied a velvet ribbon to the top.

She clasped her hands to her chest and stood back to admire the results. As she'd anticipated, the holidays brought optimism and her mood lifted.

She clicked on the stereo system she seldom used and searched for a radio station playing Christmas music. "Rockin' Around the Christmas Tree" sung by Brenda Lee, wafted through the house.

"I've never heard this version of the song," Evan noted.

She laughed. "It's one of the best, and Brenda Lee was only thirteen years old when she recorded it."

Evan foraged through a stack of boxes on the floor marked *Christmas*. "Mom, where's the ceramic nativity you painted a couple of years ago?" His voice was bubbly, his appearance relaxed.

The set, painted in a light blue, depicted Joseph, Mary, and baby Jesus.

She picked through another box. "I think I gave the set to Uncle Lincoln and Aunt Shanice."

And she remembered why. She'd intended to carve wooden dolls into a miniature nativity but never got around to it. Why couldn't time stand still? Why was she always pulled in a million directions and left the activities she enjoyed for a later time? And why did that time never come?

She surveyed the wooden dolls. They sat where Jacob had last placed them when he'd made his "house call" to check on Evan's strep throat.

A smile flickered. Jacob hadn't even seen Evan that day. He was an excellent doctor, but surely, he had come for her, and the realization brought a quiver to her heart.

Evan propped open the window seat and peered inside. "The nativity isn't in here, either." He snatched his bookbag by the stairs. "If we're done, I should go upstairs to finish my homework."

"Your hamster needs feeding," she reminded. "Tidy your room. I cleaned and straightened the house but didn't touch your room."

Audibly, he groaned. "I'm busy, Mom."

"If you want the responsibility of a puppy who requires feeding, exercise, and grooming, you must prove you're ready."

"Dr. Williams said the best time to get a dog is when a kid is eleven years old. I'm twelve, so I'm a year late already. He also said that owning a dog helps you live longer."

"You or me?"

"Both of us, I think."

"He is a fountain of information. I'm surprised either one of you gets any work done if you're chatting all the time."

"He's awesome, Mom."

Observing her son's animated expression, she knew she was running out of excuses to be upset at Jacob. Her own senseless fear of being hurt affected Evan, and he deserved the right to have a positive male role model.

Nonetheless, Jacob was a diversion, an imaginary character in her life. She'd resolved to avoid any commitments. She'd warned him that a relationship between them was out of reach. So why did thoughts of him constantly fill her mind?

In truth, he seemed hesitant, too. Sometimes, he showed more interest in Evan or the dilapidated house than in her.

She curved toward the table in the living room. Evan had homework to finish, and she had wooden dolls to carve. Another positive step in the Penelope Project. If she felt better about herself, then everything else would fall into place.

CHAPTER 8

Two weeks later, Jacob drove to Penelope's house and parked at the curb. It was a special day. It was her birthday.

He hesitated, taking in a deep breath. A beat of apprehension coursed through him. He'd taken a bold move by coming to her house, but she hadn't left him any other choice.

She'd avoided him lately, and he wasn't certain why. He'd kept his texts general, inquiring about the dilapidated house and if she had heard anything. She invariably responded by advising him to contact Candee, the realtor.

He'd boasted about Evan's ability to juggle several tasks at once when he volunteered at the clinic, and how proud she must be of him. He suggested the boy pursue other activities, too, such as choosing a favorite holiday-themed book and reading to the younger children in his school or making and sending Christmas cards to troops overseas. She'd thanked him, then told him that she and Evan participated in Toys for Tots.

I appreciate your focus on my son, but I'm his mother and have

94

things well in hand, she'd added in her text. *Oh, and I would've appreciated it if you had advised him to call me before he got into the car with Zack.*

This again? Jacob thought.

I assumed Evan would be fine, he replied. *Zack is Evan's friend, and his mother is responsible.*

Don't assume you know everything, just because you're a doctor, Penelope had countered.

Then, she had shut down the conversation.

Alrighty then. He'd nearly given up trying to get through to her. She appeared to understand the clinic's emergencies. Though how could he develop a relationship with her that had nothing to do with her son if he couldn't talk to her without her getting all offended?

Also, he'd hidden a secret, and a pain settled in the back of his throat whenever he went over his decision.

He'd opted not to tell her that he and Evan had visited the animal shelter when the clinic closed on Saturday. The shelter needed volunteers to clean cages and dog dishes, and to interact and care for the animals. Jacob and Evan also bathed and walked the dogs.

Jacob rationalized this was an important and practical first rung in Evan's learning ladder. In addition, Evan was learning more about dogs and puppies.

Well, she couldn't avoid him any longer. Fortunately, her birthday had landed on a weekday, and he figured she wouldn't celebrate until Evan arrived home from school.

He strode to the front door and rang the bell.

"Happy Birthday, beautiful," he said, when she opened the door.

Her gaze narrowed as she eyeballed the cake topper numbers on the cake he held.

"You knew I was turning fifty?" She plunked a hand on

her hip. "All I told you on the plane was that I had a birthday in November. Besides, you were sleeping."

"My eyes were half open under the sunglasses," he teased.

"So how—"

"Evan mentioned it several times. By the way, where is he?" Jacob peered toward the stairway.

"In his room, where else?" She shrugged. "He should be downstairs shortly."

"May I come in?"

"Of course." She opened the door wider and ushered him inside.

"No birthday is complete without a carrot cake topped with cream cheese frosting."

"You remembered?"

"Naturally."

"I wonder if Evan did." She preceded Jacob into the kitchen. "He's been acting awfully quiet and vague."

"He knew I was bringing the cake," Jacob confessed. "We planned your celebration ahead of time."

"When?"

"Last week." He went back to the porch, returning with a bouquet of red roses he offered her, and a six-pack of ginger beer he set on the kitchen counter. "The flowers are for you. The cake too, of course. The beer is for me. Care for a cold one?"

"No thanks." She lifted a delicate eyebrow. "How?"

"I discovered the local grocery store carries ginger beer. I opted for nonalcoholic."

"Not the beer." She shook her head. "How did you—"

He winked. "You mentioned the flowers in a text. However, lately you've become almost impossible to reach." He hoped he didn't sound overly accusing.

"I've been busy."

The age-old excuse.

He sensed her winding up more excuses and changed the topic.

"Your house looks great." The ebony-black piano gleamed, and books were stacked neatly on the coffee table. He strode into the living room, perused the stack, and held up a paperback. The front cover was a bright-blue, and a couple were in a heated embrace.

"*A Tale of a Forever Heart?*" He read the title.

She followed him. "I love sweet romance novels."

"Who is the tale about?"

"A man and a woman." She snatched the book from him and set it on top of the stack.

"Have you finished it?"

"Not this one yet. I know the ending, though."

He quirked an eyebrow. "How?"

"The sweet romances I read guarantee a happily ever after. Hearts are broken, but always mended at the end."

"You like romance."

"I love romance. The novels make me happy."

Her smile, her natural vitality and exhilaration, drew him to her. His mind drifted to the upcoming holidays and spending every waking free moment together.

On a nearby table, a line of miniature wooden dolls stood straight and colorful.

"White pants, blue coats, and red detailing," he said. "The toy soldiers are ready to march in formation. What are their names? General Admiral Oregano, Private Basil ..."

She poked him in the side. "You're a regular comedian these days."

His deep chuckle resounded through the room. "You name your wooden dolls after spices."

"You have a memory like an elephant."

"And your carved dolls are extraordinary, a work of art."

"Thank you."

She wore a short, clingy green dress that accented her figure. Her shiny hair fell to her shoulders in gentle, dark waves. She gazed at him with soulful blue eyes, a perfect complement to her light creamy complexion.

"Crikey." He almost forgot his words. "You are gorgeous, especially on your birthday."

She opened her mouth, and he held his palm up. "Don't disagree. A thank you is sufficient."

"It's not that. I've waited for you say the word *crikey*. The term is utterly Australian."

"A cultural assumption," he said. "The word is hardly used anymore by younger Australians. I'm part of the old guard."

"You and me both."

"At our age, we can leave our cares and worries behind. Now our job is to welcome our world and savor every moment."

Her full lips curved into a smile. Her dimples were adorable. "Wise words, Dr. Williams."

She was even more gorgeous when she smiled.

"I always imagined life would be better when I reached fifty," she admitted.

"It is."

"Is it?"

He bent closer to her. "Yes, because I'm here, your son is here, and we are all together."

"True."

There was no challenge in her tone, though her chin quivered, and she averted her gaze.

His heart lurched. Awareness of her sense of humor, her zest for life, shot through him. He didn't want her despondent, especially on her birthday. He felt a surge of something he'd yearned for and recognized the emotion for what it was.

Attraction. To her.

He'd left his ex-wife far behind when he'd learned of her infidelity. Since then, he'd harbored ambivalence about close relationships. He struggled, but with each passing day, realized that Penelope was the woman he could contentedly live the rest of his life with. Nevertheless, how could he overcome his uncertainties if she wouldn't allow him to get any closer?

"So, let's light the candles," he announced.

"Happy Birthday to you, Happy Birthday to you."

Jacob grinned at a smiling Penelope when he and Evan had finished singing.

"Time to blow out the candles," he teased. He'd debated placing fifty candles on the cake, but decided on the numbers five and zero, respectively.

She held back her hair, half-closed her eyes, and the two candles were extinguished in one blow.

"Hurray!" Jacob and Evan laughed and clapped.

"Mom, whose birthday comes next?" Evan asked.

"Well, yours is in February." She regarded Jacob as she began brewing coffee, then returned to the table to cut the cake. "When is your birthday?"

"January," Jacob replied.

"Really, Dr. Williams? Only a couple months away?" Evan blurted.

Jacob nodded.

"Truth?" Penelope asked Jacob skeptically. "Or did you just want the first slice of cake?"

"Truth." He offered a slight smile. "Although I'm happy to be served the first slice, regardless."

"And you'll be how old?"

"Fifty-one. Welcome to the fifties."

"I didn't realize you were older than me." Penelope

blinked, seeming to take several seconds to mentally regroup.

"Because I look so young," he joked.

"You and my mother are the same age for a few weeks!" Evan said. "Your birthday is next, Dr. Williams, so you can pull out the knife."

Jacob placed his palm over Penelope's delicate fingers. Surely, she felt the invisible magic shimmering between them. Otherwise, how could a woman's small hand push his heart into such a rapid beat?

"Make a wish." Penelope slid her hand away. "Keep it a secret or it won't come true."

Jacob closed his eyes for several seconds. "Secrets are difficult for me."

Especially when his secret wish stood directly in front of him. His feelings for her were shattering any final reservations. The awareness seemed sudden because he'd only met her a few short months ago.

He sat on a chair, cracked open a ginger beer, and downed half.

"No coffee?" she asked.

"I'll stick with beer."

He needed something to quell his nerves. Lately, he couldn't sleep, pondering his feelings. Could he get married again at his age? Penelope was a divorcee with a preteen boy. In the past, he'd stepped away from any conflicts. He'd attended college rather than deal with his family. Their problems and goals were too different from his. Same was true of his hospital job in Atlanta. However, he believed his decision to relocate to Roses was the right choice, and the reason was standing in the same room.

Penelope poured herself a cup of coffee and sat across from him. "Earth to Jacob Williams," she said.

"Sorry. I was thinking."

"About?"

"Your festive home." He gestured toward the living room. "The decorated tree inspires me. I wish the holidays were already here."

"I love Christmas." Despite her words, her eyes were sad.

"Me too."

"Me three," Evan chimed in. "Mom, did Dr. Williams tell you he plans to dress up as Santa Claus at the clinic next month?"

"No, he didn't." She plated a heaping slice of cake for each of them while Evan rummaged in the freezer for a carton of chocolate ice cream.

"I thought it would be fun for the kids," Jacob said, "though I haven't found a Santa costume yet."

"You will," she replied. "The children will call you Doc Christmas."

"I love Christmas," he repeated.

"Bah, humbug," she half joked. "You're Doc Christmas but sometimes I feel like I'm Mrs. Scrooge."

"Dr. Williams, did my mom mention we are spending Thanksgiving on Uncle Lincoln's houseboat on Hilton Head Island?" Evan brought the carton of ice cream to the table. "Our neighbor watches my hamster when we go away. When I get my puppy, we'll take my puppy with us."

"Oh, we will, will we?" Penelope crossed her arms.

"If my mother says it's okay, you can join us. Unless you have other plans." Evan beamed at Jacob, then glanced at Penelope.

"I don't have anything special planned." Jacob set down his fork. *Whoa. Wait. Wasn't a houseboat a boat on the ocean? Since his niece's accident, he'd avoided pools and lakes. This scenario was even scarier. This was an ocean.*

A smile flickered across Penelope's face. "Of course, you're invited, Jacob."

"Are you staying all week? I'm working until Wednesday." Inwardly, he grappled with his words. He wanted to celebrate Thanksgiving with them, but a houseboat wasn't part of the equation. Somewhere on land, a cabin, for instance, sounded infinitely better, and much safer. "I always phone my mum and my sister on holidays."

She scooped ice cream onto each plate and handed him and Evan a spoon.

"Call them from the houseboat," she replied.

"You have cell phone service?"

"The boat isn't sailing anywhere because it's not motorized. It stays in one place—docked at the marina. Water and sewer and electricity are provided by the shore power. Houseboat living is like staying at a vacation home. Do you swim?"

"Why?" He tilted his head and tried to contain his shudder. "Will I need to?"

"Not unless you want to."

"I'm not a strong swimmer."

"You won't need to wear a life jacket while you eat Thanksgiving dinner." She grinned. "The boat hardly sways."

"Hardly." He blew out a speculative breath and met her gaze. "I'll make a deal."

"What kind?"

"While I'm talking to my mum and sister, I'll introduce you and turn the phone over to you."

"Fine. I'm thrilled to chat with them both."

He gave an ironic laugh. "You're in for an adventure."

Boy, was she ever.

She wandered to the sink to wipe her hands on a dishtowel, then stepped to him. "You're completely off work for a few days?"

"I'm close enough to Roses to drive back if there is an emergency, though Dr. Hannaway, the town GP, is taking on extra shifts as we've expanded. Even though we have different specialties, the limited number of doctors here makes it possible for us to cover for each other if needed. She's excellent and no-nonsense. Plus, we use each other as a sounding board." He hesitated. "The drive from Hilton Head to Roses is what ... around three hours?"

"Depending on traffic. I imagine the Thanksgiving holiday is busy at a clinic."

"Most common is a condition doctors call holiday heart." He finger quoted. At her curious expression, he explained. "It's caused by excessive drinking. The patient usually comes in pale and sweaty and smelling of alcohol."

"Is the condition serious?"

"It can be, if heart palpitations are rapid."

"Let's pray no one sees any of that," she said.

Evan piped in after he'd finished the cake and ice cream on his plate. "Can we take a ferryboat to Daufuskie Island for the day? The trip is short from Hilton Head."

"We'd have to ride on another boat to get there?" Jacob inquired.

"The ferry is small, Dr. Williams."

Jacob scraped a hand through his hair. Irrational thoughts flooded his brain. Suppose there was a strong wind and the small boat overturned?

"Not everyone is comfortable on boats," Penelope replied to Evan. "Each of us wrestle with our own fears." She nodded conspiratorially at Jacob. An understanding nod, and he tipped his head back to take in her sweet face. "My fear is planes."

He smiled. "I remember."

"Lincoln and Shanice won't be around, as they're taking an extended holiday," Penelope went on. "They hardly use the houseboat anymore. Did you know my brother is also an author?"

"What does he write?"

"Children's books. *Tuggy the Tugboat* books are his best-loved series, which is the main reason why he wants to hold on to the boat."

Jacob downed the rest of his ginger beer. "Which is?"

"Inspiration, I imagine." She sat again and sipped her coffee. "The weeks between Thanksgiving and Christmas are hectic for toy shops. I'm spending hours ordering inventory and managing invoices. Fortunately, our employees are more than capable, though with Lincoln gone, I'll be on call if anything goes wrong."

A wide grin spread across Evan's face. "We'll decorate the houseboat for Christmas. Wait till you see how we tape red stockings to the kitchen cabinets, Dr. Williams. Uncle Lincoln has an artificial pine tree in a storage unit, and we hang tinsel everywhere." Evan placed his dish in the sink and bounded toward the hall. "We also cut out paper snowflakes for the boat's windows. Don't we, Mom?"

Before Penelope answered, Evan skipped up the stairs.

"Lots of sparkle and flair." Jacob offered a bemused smile.

"This entire conversation has caught me by surprise." Penelope returned to the sink and began loading the dishwasher.

"Which part?" Jacob placed his bottle in the kitchen's recycling bin. "The paper snowflakes?"

"Not funny."

"Have I been uninvited for Thanksgiving?"

"You're still invited. A deal is a deal."

"You'll cook a turkey?"

"Roger's Diner, my favorite restaurant on the island, offers a spectacular takeout spread. The entire turkey with all the trimmings. I don't cook large meals on the boat, because the oven heats up the boat too quickly. However, there is a full kitchen, complete with a stove, refrigerator, and microwave."

Jacob strode close to her, the delicate floral whiff of lavender flooding his nostrils. The scent was calming, lightening his mood, and quelling his reservations about a sinking houseboat.

Her back was to him, and he wrapped his arms around her waist. "I missed you," he whispered in her ear.

"Yet here I am."

"I tried texting."

Her lips pursed. "Busy," she murmured.

"Are you still upset about the accident with Zack and his mother?"

"I was concerned and worried."

"I hope you don't blame me. I got caught up with patients and—"

"Don't be silly."

"However, you've avoided me."

"Busy," she repeated.

"My birthday girl has a lot of the same excuses I don't buy."

She tilted her head toward him. Her lips were slightly parted. "What don't you buy?"

The expression on her features mirrored his own, confirming his feelings. Her eyes were teasing and appraising, and his pulse thrummed a steady beat. In that moment, he realized she cared for him as much as he cared for her.

"Your excuses for avoiding me," he said. "I forgive you. Please forgive me."

"Of course." She inhaled and turned to him. "Jacob, whatever you're thinking … this isn't a good idea."

"The best idea I've had in a long time." He cradled her face in his hands and kissed her gently and thoroughly. "In fact, I have an even better idea."

She gazed up at him. "I can only imagine."

"No more of this "undate" stuff. From now on, we're officially dating. We're a couple."

She trembled in his arms, slightly, as if he had stirred an emotion she was trying to suppress. "Promise me you'll never turn into a Roy."

He wanted to bury his lips in the curve of her neck. She brought gladness and love into his life. She was fresh and vibrant, witty, and delightful.

"I promise." He sealed his assurance with an affirming kiss.

CHAPTER 9

A houseboat wasn't Jacob's idea of the ideal place to observe an American Thanksgiving. First and foremost, he was petrified of being on a boat.

Okay, not petrified. Just not totally comfortable swinging back and forth on a floating "vacation home."

The America part? He loved the country and was thrilled to celebrate the traditional holiday. After relocating, his family had become US citizens, and he appreciated having dual citizenship for both Australia and the United States.

At present, totally stuffed from Thanksgiving dinner, he placed his cloth napkin to the side and pushed back from the galley table. "Best meal I've ever had, and so much food it took two hands to carry the turkey platter to the table. My compliments to Chef Roger."

"I doubt the diner is still owned by a guy named Roger," Penelope replied.

"At least the cooks carried on Roger's legacy." Jacob patted his stomach appreciatively. "Especially the mashed potatoes with loads of butter."

Seemingly caught between laughter and agreement, she smiled and didn't protest.

"If we're done, I'll get the Christmas trimmings." Evan's face flushed with excitement. "Mom and I hauled the tree out of storage before you came on board, Dr. Williams, but there are plenty of decorations left."

Penelope gazed out the window. "The unit is on the other side of the marina."

"I know where it is, Mom. We've been here a thousand times."

"Soon, it will be dark," she said.

"Yeah, in like three hours."

"Go ahead, then." She clutched her hands together. "We'll finish cleaning, and when you return, let's start trimming the boat for Christmas."

After Evan shrugged on his leather jacket and skipped out the door, Jacob pulled her into his arms. A flow of heat passed between them, a crackle of attraction he couldn't deny. Her heady feminine fragrance called for a kiss.

"Thank you for a wonderful Thanksgiving," he said.

She licked her lips and regarded him with unabashed affection. "My pleasure."

Those lips. A rosy tint from his kisses enhanced her full mouth. He'd be thinking about those lips all evening.

He sighed and glanced at his watch. "This may be a good time to phone my mum."

Penelope brought their dishes to the sink. "Do you want some privacy?"

"No." He stepped to her, claimed her hand, and squeezed. "You're part of the deal."

"Are we video chatting with her?"

Curtly, he shook his head. "A phone call is sufficient."

Jacob peered around, admiring the boat's interior. Penelope had explained her brother had opted for white paint to make the space look bigger. The open floor plan on the upper deck featured a dining room, kitchen, and living room, and the reclaimed wooden floors were originally crafted and removed from an old school. The lower deck offered bedrooms, three bedroom, two full-sized bathrooms, and a half bath. In total, the houseboat was two thousand square feet.

The ocean views from the docked boat were jaw-dropping. Waves swished, and the cries of seagulls squawked as their wings beat through the air.

With his duffle bag slung over his shoulder, he'd admired the gorgeous wooden and rope walkway when he'd arrived. The handmade door boasted an antique porthole. "I didn't envision this type of luxury," he admitted.

"*Shay's Secret*." He'd read the boat's name engraved over the entry and asked, "Who is Shay?"

"Shanice. Lincoln's wife," Penelope said. "Shay is his nickname for her."

"What's her secret?"

"They have a history together. They dated in college and then broke up. She left him because of our father, who didn't approve of their relationship. She never explained her reasons to Lincoln. Fortunately, they ended up finding each other again in Roses and thus, true love."

"The best kind." Jacob offered a nod of approval. "Just like your romance novels."

On Thanksgiving morning, he'd woken to a golden sunrise streaming into his bedroom window. He'd stepped outside and relaxed on the deck while savoring a cup of fresh-brewed coffee. The mouthwatering scents of roasted turkey, sweet potatoes, cranberry sauce, and warm-from-the-oven bread filled his nostrils.

"Smells like turkey day!" Evan exclaimed, and Jacob heartily concurred.

Now as he rinsed dishes, a cloud of impending doom descended over him as he anticipated the upcoming call.

"I'd prefer you're here with me when I phone my mum." He wiped his hands on a dishtowel and started toward the living room sofa with Penelope. He beckoned her to sit next to him and she complied, snuggling against his shoulder. He smiled down at her, and his breath quickened at the delightful sensation of her closeness. He drew her tighter and pressed a kiss on her lips. Her gaze lifted to meet his, and the gentle yielding in her magnificent eyes almost made him forget about the dreaded upcoming phone call altogether. He wanted to keep Penelope in his arms forever.

She'd taken extra pains with her appearance and wore a cable knit blue sweater dress. Cozy, yet casual, the dress enhanced her smooth complexion, and her dark hair shone in the afternoon sunlight.

Jacob had opted for jeans and a chambray shirt.

"Don't you want to talk to your family alone first?" Penelope asked.

"Nope." Jacob loosened his hold around her shoulders, fighting the impulse to keep her as near as possible. "My mum is ... well ... my mum. Our relationship is rocky, at best."

"What about your sister?"

"Kylie has had a hard go of it these past few years. She's been angry with me, though we've begun to mend our fences."

"Part of your long, tragic story?" Penelope inquired.

"The very same." He responded with a small nod. "Kylie is considering moving back to Australia."

"With your mother?"

"Possibly." He studied his cell phone, as if searching for answers. "My mum can't handle all the farm chores on her own, though my sister has frequently helped. However, now that Kylie and her husband have split, only the two women are holding onto an old, rundown farm."

"You seem to gravitate toward rundown things yourself."

"Or rush away from them. I apparently have a love-hate relationship going." He narrowed his eyes. "Are you trying to analyze me?"

"I have enough on my plate trying to analyze myself."

He hesitated. Should he phone his mother now, or wait a bit? Speaking about his mother revealed his ambivalence more than he realized.

There was no time like the present, he encouraged himself. Rubbing a hand over his jaw, he clicked on her number.

"Hello?" an elderly woman's voice answered.

"Happy Thanksgiving, Mum," Jacob began.

"Who is this?"

"Your son, Jacob."

"Nice of you to remember your mum and ring me once in a while."

"I call you every week and text whenever I can." He gave himself a small shake. "Happy Thanksgiving."

"We're not American, Jacob."

"We've lived in the States longer than Australia and we're American citizens." A familiar emptiness overwhelmed him. No matter what he achieved, he could never please her.

He peered at the stereo system in the corner. Perhaps if he was armed with relaxing music in the background, the music would subdue his anxiousness instead of being surrounded by silence. As if reading his mind, Penelope grabbed a remote. She tuned into a station of holiday classics, and "Oh Come, All Ye Faithful" sounded, sung by a male choir.

He gazed at her, curled up on the sofa beside him. She

looked the opposite of how he felt. Her features were determined and resilient.

His protector.

He smiled at that. Penelope, rising to his defense in any storm.

"Are you working today at your fancy clinic?" his mother inquired.

"Another doctor is on call, Mum. And you're confusing the clinic with the hospital in Atlanta."

"Are you all moved into your new place?"

"I'm renting an apartment. I'd love if you visited me for the holidays."

"You're a big shot doctor. You don't have time for your mother."

"I have plenty of time for you, mum." He pressed his lips tightly together.

"You didn't have time for the farm. It could've collapsed all around you and you wouldn't have cared."

"I'm not a farmer. I wanted to be a doctor and I couldn't turn down the full scholarship for being valedictorian of my class. Besides, I want to help people."

"Doesn't charity begin at home?"

His stomach churned, and he reached for the glass of water Penelope had placed next to him. "Did you receive my check this month?"

"The money was a little less than usual."

"I'm sorry. The clinic was more expensive to start up than I anticipated, and coupled with the expense of moving from Atlanta and buying another doctor's practice ..."

He rubbed his forehead, then slung an arm around Penelope's shoulders. "Look, the weather is warmer in the Carolinas than in Maryland. Roses sponsors a Christmas parade and features a holiday sing-along concert in the park."

"I like snow at Christmas."

"I haven't lived here long enough to forecast for sure." He glanced at Penelope. "I'm certain they get snow sometimes."

"Sometimes," she mouthed.

"I prefer a white Christmas," his mother said.

He sank deeper into the sofa. He'd had this type of discussion often and instructed himself to remain upbeat. Nonetheless, if he liked red, his mum would say the opposite and like blue. The past was a mere breath away, and he clearly sensed this conversation was resembling all the others.

"I'm considering purchasing a home in Roses and setting up my practice in the house." He struggled to find the right words to describe his dream. "It needs work, but the house has character."

"Our farm has character."

"Is Kylie there?" He briefly closed his eyes. "She is welcome to visit for Christmas, too."

"She's busy in the kitchen and can't talk."

"Some other time, then. Please wish her a lovely Thanksgiving." He sat still for a moment. "Mum, I'd like to introduce you to a very special someone. I'm officially dating a wonderful woman, and her name is Penelope. She wants to say hello."

"Now?" Penelope whispered.

He nodded vigorously.

She rubbed the back of her neck, then accepted his cell phone. She exchanged light pleasantries with his mother, then handed the phone to him for a final goodbye.

When he clicked off, he leaned back against the sofa. Still holding Penelope close, his body sagged.

Some conversations rendered people speechless. This conversation with his mum was one of them.

CHAPTER 10

"'Deck the halls with boughs of holly.'" The following morning, Evan belted out the carol in a faultless tenor voice while he taped paper Christmas stockings to the kitchen cabinets. His wide beam of delight lit his entire face.

Penelope grinned. She loved seeing him happy. These were precious memories she'd tuck away and revisit forever. These were the festive times chipping away at her insecurities and resentments toward her ex. These moments brought optimism for a brilliant future.

She'd picked out a pair of linen joggers and a dazzling red sweater. She'd decided to grow out her hair, and loose brown waves framed her face. She'd parted her hair in a deep side part.

She followed Evan into the living room, where Jacob, squatting on the floor, was setting up a three-foot artificial tree. The scents of a Christmas candle, balsam pine and cedar, wafted through the air.

"Can I ask you a question, Penelope?" Jacob stood, his tall, commanding frame dwarfing the tree. He brushed silver tinsel off his jeans, though tinsel still stuck to his hair and green polo shirt.

"Sure." She smothered a giggle and reached up to pluck the tinsel from his hair. "Are you planning to turn into a Christmas tree?"

"I'm Doctor Santa, remember?" He brushed the tinsel from his shirt. "When is the soup done?"

"A few more hours. It's simmering on the stove."

Earlier in the morning, she and Jacob had picked over the turkey carcass, then sliced extra vegetables—onions, carrots, and celery—to a turkey broth. A rice cooker supplied the rice they would add later.

"Smells homey and delicious." He stepped toward the kitchen and sniffed the heavenly aroma. "All we need is a bag of sticky caramel corn to munch on while we binge watch holiday movies. I vote for *National Lampoon's Christmas Vacation.*"

Evan fixed a sparkling white angel to the top of the tree. "That movie is one of my favorites. Let's stream it tonight."

Penelope stood back to admire the decorations. An eclectic mix of humorous, stylish, and handmade ornaments brought a fun, understated elegance to the boat. It was a shame, she thought, that she wouldn't be back here to enjoy the festive ambiance. However, Lincoln and Shanice declared that they would stay on the houseboat in January and celebrate the holidays then.

By late morning, red and green bulbs sparkled around the fake fireplace, and a blinking *Ho, Ho, Ho* sign hung over the corner bar. Penelope hadn't observed a true, merry Christmas since her divorce. However, she imagined the upcoming weeks with Jacob as picture-perfect opportunities to awaken her sense of joyousness in the season.

As if reading her thoughts, he reached for her hand and gave a light squeeze. His warm smile filled with love.

Love. For her. The thought brought unexpected flutters to her chest.

"Can I play video games in my bedroom?" Evan asked when he finished hanging the last strand of tinsel on the tree.

"Sure." Penelope turned to Jacob and reciprocated his smile. "Thanks for all your decorating help."

"You're very welcome," he replied. "My pleasure."

"Later I want to go swimming," Evan said. "I brought my swimsuit."

"Swimming?" She expressed her disbelief aloud. Evan hadn't asked to swim in months. "The water is cold." She hesitated to say more, though she didn't wish to discourage him, especially with Jacob staring at her.

A wistful look crossed Evan's face. "I'll just take a quick dip."

"Not in the marina," she replied. "Long gone are the days when you can jump in from the boat. This water is dangerous with electricity and fumes and operators unable to see you." Her hands gripped the chair, a myriad of accidents that might await Evan flashing through her mind. "There are *No Swimming* signs posted everywhere, and any further discussion on this subject is nonnegotiable."

"Message received, Mom. You've given me a thousand lectures about the dangers, but Pelican Beach is a short walk from here. I'm a strong swimmer. So are you. Come with me."

"I'll pass."

"What about you, Dr. Williams?" Evan asked.

Jacob's entire body stiffened. "Your mother and I will sit and chat." With that, he led her to the outdoor deck overlooking the harbor.

The view of the ocean beyond was spectacular, and she'd noted he'd taken in every detail of the houseboat, both inside and out.

"In December, the holiday lights take to the water," she said. "Hilton Head holds a twinkling boat parade."

Jacob raised a dark eyebrow. "Sounds marvelous if I can watch from the shore. However, if you invite me, then I'll be there."

They stood by the handrails, an ocean breeze cooling her cheeks.

He wrapped an arm around her. "Simply breathtaking," he breathed, as he gazed down at her face. The same breeze ruffled his dark, thick hair as he studied the sunlight glinting off the water, then contemplated the sapphire blue sky.

He looked incredibly handsome, and nothing took away from the peacefulness and pleasure of standing with this conscientious, dashing man. Earlier, he'd jogged around the marina shirtless, and she'd admired his hard chest and flat stomach as sweat pooled along his muscular arms. After returning to the houseboat and showering, he'd responded to numerous phone calls from his staff. He'd assured Penelope that Thanksgiving at the clinic had been thankfully without any alarming incidents, save for grease burns from frying a turkey, upset stomachs from overeating, and a bout of food poisoning.

"Dr. Hannaway is keeping an eye on a holiday heart patient," he said. "She's monitoring his abnormal heart rhythm."

"Is she on call the entire weekend?" Penelope asked.

"Yes. This weekend is officially my vacation. However, I'm scheduled to work at the clinic on Christmas Eve day and on Christmas Day."

"Perfect for your Santa outfit," she teased.

He chuckled. "Meanwhile, how is the toy business?"

"We fussed with our window display, and it features a lighted carousel and several handmade elf puppets. I insisted on background Christmas music to be played in the store."

"Is "Jingle Bells" the standard fare?"

"Jesus is the reason for the season, and I prefer to keep Christ in Christmas. So, "Oh, Little Town of Bethlehem" is perfect."

"I agree." He rubbed his thumb over her wrist and kissed her hand. "In addition, I like giving and receiving gifts, too."

Her hand tingled from his warm lips. "We also devoted one floor of the shop to wooden rocking horses in all shapes and sizes. There's a rocking horse convention this weekend and a couple of busloads of people are expected to tour our store."

"There's such a thing as a rocking horse convention?"

"Apparently." Penelope had checked with several of her toy shops and the holiday season was off to a promising start. Lincoln had texted from New York City and declared that he and Shay were having a splendid time seeing the famous sights.

"This is the first year Lincoln and Shanice won't be hosting a Christmas party," Penelope mused.

"I'll host a Christmas party," Jacob said.

"You will?"

"Absolutely." He searched her face. "Will you attend?"

"I'd love to."

"Good. I'm throwing a Polar Express party at the clinic and will serve hot chocolate. I requested new sleepwear donations for the children, and the outreach from the community has been overwhelming."

"Another advantage of living in Roses." Grinning, she settled on a deep-cushioned teak love seat and Jacob nestled beside her. He looped an arm around her shoulders, and her heart leapt in her chest when he nuzzled her neck. A glow of exhilaration and affection surged through her.

"This is a wonderful life," he whispered as his lips gravitated to hers. "The island is genuinely peaceful. A real corker."

"Corker?" She gave him her undivided attention. "What's that mean?"

"Australian slang for really good, mate." His eyes gleamed wickedly, and she couldn't prevent a broad smile from spreading across her face.

"This entire harbor will decorate for Christmas," she said. "Red bows on all the lanterns, and many owners will string colored lights on their boats." Her gaze roamed over the glistening water. Smooth waves followed various boats as they motored out of the harbor.

She inhaled. A whiff of salty air never failed to invigorate her.

"Why are people drawn to the water?" she mused.

"Some people," Jacob corrected with a grim smile.

She looked up at him. "What do you mean?"

"Some people are, some people aren't."

"You mentioned you aren't a strong swimmer."

He shrugged indifferently. "I can hold my own. I'm not a champion like you or your son."

"We've grown up around the water."

"Crikey, I'm an Aussie guy." He broke out in his thickest Australian accent. "My family's farm in Maryland isn't near the sea."

Penelope stood to check the soup.

"There's something I want to tell you." His gaze pinned to hers. "My story involves swimming."

Her chest tensed at his serious tone, and her voice rose in pitch. "What is it?"

"Sit for a while longer." He patted the seat and pulled her back down beside him. "I'm ready for you to hear my long, tragic tale."

By his decree, she'd assumed the subject was closed and shot him a questioning glance. "Truth?" she inquired.

"Always. You're a good listener."

"I try." He leaned back against the cushions and stretched out his long, muscular legs.

"At least when I'm not talking constantly." She managed to keep her tone joking to lighten his suddenly pensive mood.

He inhaled a lengthy breath and then released it. "My sister, Kylie, had a daughter."

Had. Penelope noted the past tense and her heart constricted.

"Linda," she said. "You mentioned she never fully recovered. What happened?"

"A swimming accident when she was young. She nearly drowned."

"How old was she?"

"She was in elementary school. The accident occurred in a friend's pool. My sister sat by the pool and looked away for a few seconds when Linda suddenly went under the water. Kylie dove in and rescued her, and her quick thinking saved her daughter. However, Linda's brain suffered from a lack of oxygen. The doctor in our little town diagnosed the injury as not severe."

Penelope reached out and patted his hand.

"The doctor was wrong." Despite Jacob's somber expression, his voice remained calm. "Linda began having seizures. A couple years ago, she took a turn for the worse and suffered from amnesia and muscle spasms before she died."

His voice cracked, bringing tears to Penelope's eyes. "Jacob, I'm so sorry."

"I miss my sweet niece. We all do." He shuddered, as if a memory from the past was ever present. "Kylie was an excellent caregiver."

Penelope's stomach twisted in a sharp knot. "The ... the remembrances must be difficult for you to process and—"

"I was working in Atlanta and left as soon as my sister phoned." His gaze focused on the horizon, where the water met the sky. His voice trailed off. "I didn't arrive in Maryland on time."

"I'm certain you got there quickly."

He bit down on his bottom lip, seeming to ponder his next words. "Not quickly enough. Kylie never forgave me. She never forgave me for not being at the pool that day, either. I had visited for the weekend but had stayed back to lend a hand on the farm."

"Don't blame yourself. There was nothing you could do in either case." Penelope swallowed as the risk of tears passed and the thickness in her throat began to dissolve.

"Explain that to my sister. I'm a doctor. I should've been able to do something."

"She'll come around eventually." Penelope still reeled, and her tears flowed again. Her heart ached for Jacob and Kylie, and his family. She pictured his niece, perhaps with the same dark hair and deep-brown eyes as he had.

"Continue to reach out to your sister," she said, dabbing at her wet cheeks.

"I will. Since then, I've been uncomfortable around the water. Coupled with the difficult memories, the dangers seem more pronounced than ever." He touched one of Penelope's tears with his fingertip. "Thank you for listening. Thank you for caring."

She gazed up at him, surprised at his heartfelt thanks. She wasn't accustomed to a man who wore his feelings on his sleeve. She wasn't accustomed to the emotions he woke inside her.

They sat for several minutes, watching the hypnotic rise

and fall of the ocean, and she burrowed her face against his chest.

So that explained why his expression had paled when she'd mentioned the houseboat. He'd been leery, cautious, and a bit skittish. Now she understood why.

A while later, her cell phone buzzed, and she recognized the number immediately. *Roses Toy Shop*. The manager was capable and would only phone if an emergency arose.

She stood. "Jacob, I apologize. I have to take this call."

"We lost power on the street because a transformer went out," her manager began without preamble when she clicked on. "Two busloads of folks from the Rocking Horse event are scheduled to pull up within the next few hours."

"Are you closing the store?"

"We plan to stay open, although it's dark here with no lights. I sent the staff out for flashlights, though I anticipate cash register sales will be a challenge."

"Thankfully, it's daylight," she replied. "Do you want me to come help?"

"We're shorthanded and the rain is coming down in sheets," the manager said. "Our parking lot is tight, and someone needs to direct traffic."

Mentally, Penelope estimated the time it took to drive to Roses. Three hours. The store was open until eight o'clock, though they might close early once darkness fell. Still, she'd be able to assist for a good portion of the day.

"I should leave now," she murmured, half to herself.

"Leave?" Jacob was on his feet. "Where? Why?"

"The toy shop in Roses." She rubbed her palms across her linen joggers and irritably shook her head. Her job was interfering with a wonderful weekend, although she had no choice. Her business came first, particularly during the holidays, and especially with Lincoln out of town.

"The shop lost power because a transformer is out in the area," she said. "The staff is buying every flashlight in sight."

"What can I do?" Jacob asked.

She stared blankly out at the ocean. "Will you stay with Evan? And stir the soup?"

His lips formed a smile as he placed his hands on her shoulders. "Whatever helps."

"Thanks." She rushed inside the houseboat to grab her keys and shrug on a cotton jacket. "I'll direct cars in the toy shop's parking lot. Believe me, in the pouring rain it's the job no one else wants. I'm the owner, and I must lead by example."

"You're a professional and selfless woman and absolutely amazing."

"I hate leaving Evan."

She also hated leaving Jacob.

"Evan is fine." Jacob clasped her cold hands. "We'll play board games, walk the marina, and eat soup. Tonight, we'll watch the movie, unless you want us to wait for you."

"Don't. Sounds like a plan." She turned toward the stairs and called out. "Evan, I'm driving to Roses but should return around ten. Dr. Williams is here."

"Awesome," came the quick response.

"Drive carefully," Jacob said. Their gazes met and held. He hugged her, and she relished the solidness of his muscles, the warmth of his hands on her back heating her insides. He brought "tidings of comfort and joy," like the lyrics of her favorite Christmas carol, "God Rest Ye, Merry Gentlemen." Her breath paused for a beat at the wonder of Jacob's embrace, the wonder of *him* to make everything right.

"I'll keep your son safe," he promised, pressing a tender kiss on her lips.

He made her feel sheltered and adored, and nothing could

dampen her excitement at the upcoming weeks with him by her side.

Because nothing was as important as security and ... love.

Willfully, she lifted her chin. Love was the last feeling she wanted, and contemplations along those lines only betrayed her. Still, what was more exhilarating than love, especially during the most magical season of the year?

She refused to feign indifference to him any longer. If anything, she cared for him more than she ever dreamed possible.

"No reservations about leaving Evan," she reassured herself as she withdrew from Jacob's hold. As she walked along the narrow dock to the parking lot, she scuffed at a shiny pebble in her path. "My son is in Jacob's capable hands," she said aloud. "What could possibly go wrong?"

CHAPTER 11

$\mathcal{J}$acob strode into the kitchen as soon as Penelope left. He stirred the turkey soup simmering on the stove and sipped a spoonful. Savory and delicious, and he sprinkled a dash of salt and pepper into the broth.

Penelope had placed the rice cooker, a box of rice, and a measuring cup on the counter.

He grinned. She was certainly a planner, and wow, did she look gorgeous. She was everything he could ever ask for. Efficient, brilliant, and stunning. Was that why he couldn't form a coherent thought whenever she entered a room?

"Dr. Williams, I'm going swimming," Evan announced. He emerged from his bedroom and bound into the kitchen wearing swimming trunks, sandals, and a faded T-shirt, with a towel thrown over his shoulder.

Jacob checked his watch. The time showed past noon, and Penelope had most likely driven over the bridge connecting Hilton Head Island to the mainland and was well on her way to Roses. A glance out the window promised blue skies and a clear afternoon.

"Where are you swimming?" Jacob placed the spoon on a spoon rest on top of the stove.

"Pelican Beach. It isn't far." Evan bobbed toward the window and pointed to a sandy beach beyond. "My mother said it was okay."

"I'll walk with you." Jacob covered the soup pan with a lid and turned off the stove.

"Did you bring a swimsuit, Dr. Williams?"

"No." Nor did he ever intend to swim again if he could help it, Jacob thought. He stepped to the closet and retrieved a beach towel, then two water bottles from the refrigerator. "I'll sit on the sand and watch you."

They hiked through a stretch of pine trees and a planked wooden path and soon arrived at Pelican Beach. High grass grew between silky, golden sand dunes. Waves crashed against the rocks. A field boasted yellow and pink wildflowers.

Evan paused to pick up fragments of seashells and flat stones, then shook off his sandals. Jacob followed suit, and they fell into step across the wet sand as they neared the ocean.

Jacob scanned the beach, deserted except for a young couple cuddling, and a child digging in the sand. A scattering of fishing boats anchored in the distance.

"No lifeguard?" he inquired.

"In November, not many people are at the beach," Evan replied. "Plus, this beach is hidden from the main boardwalk. Only the locals realize it isn't private and open to everyone. My mother can probably walk to every inlet blindfolded because Grandma and Grandpa lived here."

The ocean was an exceptional turquoise-blue, and the sun lit the water all a glitter. Jacob tasted the briny tang of salt and vegetation on his tongue.

Yes, this glorious island was a beaut, and his insides gave

a peculiar little lurch. Hilton Head was a second home for Penelope, and he envisioned her as a young girl, sunburned and giggling while creating castles in the sand or swimming in the ocean.

"Mom loves the beach," Evan said.

"I can see why." A cool breeze whipped across Jacob's face as he smoothed out his towel and sat. "The sea is a magical place."

"She is a champion swimmer. She swam often when we lived in Virginia."

"Not anymore?" Jacob peered upward as several seagulls circled overhead, then flew past.

"Not since we moved to Roses. In Virginia, my mother was fearless. I remember going camping with my parents and she dove into deep lakes without thinking twice." Evan set his towel on the sand beside Jacob and pulled off his T-shirt. "Now she worries all the time. Take today, for instance."

"You asked if you could swim, and she didn't argue."

"Yeah, but she always frets about the tide pulling me under the water. I remind her I'm careful and not afraid and it doesn't do any good."

Jacob feigned polite applause. "Well, I, for one, approve of your bravery."

"Can I tell you something else, Dr. Williams?"

"Certainly."

"My mom seems happier now that you two are dating. I think this Thanksgiving is the best weekend of her life. Mine too!" Evan chugged from his water bottle, set the bottle on his towel, then headed for the ocean.

"Don't go far." Jacob pulled his knees to his chest. The weather proved cooler than he'd anticipated, and he shivered, regretting not bringing a jacket.

Evan stood by the shore before taking tentative steps, then splashing in the surf. "The water is cold!" he shouted.

"I can only imagine," Jacob said. His thoughts curved to Penelope. He'd risked exposing his vulnerability, showing emotion regarding his difficult relationships with his mum and sister. The loss of his sweet niece. Penelope was kind and gracious and seemed to absorb his sadness and blame.

Were introductions between his mum and Penelope over the phone the right approach? He wanted her to meet his family, assuming they would grow to love her as much as he did. A phone chat was a start.

Whoa. Backpedal. *Love.* He'd vowed never to fall in love again. He enjoyed dating, but one heartbreaking devastation in his life was enough. When had love come into play?

His thoughts shied away from studying his feelings too intently. After his divorce, he had little confidence in his ability to judge his emotions.

You fell in love with Penelope the first day you met her on the plane, his conscience prompted. She was brave and captivating, ambitious, and loving.

Not far away, Evan waded farther into the water and then dove in. With a deliberate scissoring of his legs, he swam forward, then drifted and floated on his back.

The wind whipped up, and Jacob stood, tucking the beach towel over his shoulders. If the air was cold, the ocean in November must be bone-chilling.

"Aren't you freezing?" he shouted to Evan.

Evan turned, but apparently didn't hear Jacob. The boy paddled to a rocky shore in an inlet, found a sunny spot, and sat beneath a ledge.

"Smart kid," Jacob muttered, seeking a sunny location on the sand for himself. His cell phone buzzed, and he yanked it from his pocket, assuming Penelope might be calling.

Instead, the phone number from the clinic floated across his screen.

"Dr. Williams?" a woman inquired when he answered.

"Hello, Dr. Hannaway." He recognized the woman's voice.

"Our holiday heart patient is complaining of chest pain," she said.

"What's the patient's age?"

"The man is in his sixties."

The wind picked up and the percussive sounds of the waves hitting the shore grew louder.

"His heart rhythm hasn't stabilized?" Jacob pressed the phone closer to his ear, turned away from Evan, and focused on the sand to concentrate. He noted that the young couple and the child had disappeared.

"His heartbeat is more rapid."

Jacob gnawed his bottom lip and weighed the options. "Let's use a beta blocker to slow the heart rate."

"I agree. Thank you," Dr. Hannaway replied.

Jacob clicked off and twisted back to view Evan.

The boy waved, then climbed higher on the rocks. The kid was adventurous, and Jacob debated whether he should discourage him.

When Evan neared the top of the ledge, Jacob watched in mounting fear. "That's far enough. The peak is too high!" Panic rose in his throat. Surely the rocks were slick.

"I'm okay. I'm gonna jump. I've done this before." Evan slipped and righted himself, then swiveled toward the water and stretched out his arms.

Weighed down by dread, a knot twisted in Jacob's gut.

"Don't!"

Afterwards, Jacob couldn't remember if his shout had been loud enough to carry.

A split-second later, Evan dove in.

All was quiet.

Jacob stood stock still, frozen in horror. Surely Evan would quickly break the surface and tread water. Uneasiness poured along his spine.

Drowning. His niece. Not again.

Twice, he hadn't been there to save Linda. But he would save Evan.

He could swim. Not great, but enough.

He cast his gaze across the shore. Still no sign of Evan.

Fear spiked. Time sped up, though his movements seemed to slow down.

No. He refused to be paralyzed. He flung his towel to the sand and raced toward the ocean.

RELIEVED that the power to the toy shop had been restored, Penelope hummed the melody of "Angels We Have Heard on High." A tabernacle choir belted the carol from her truck's radio as she headed back toward Hilton Head. The manager had phoned, and everything was under control.

As she stepped into the houseboat, she was still humming the carol. "Surprise! I'm back!" she called out.

Hmm. Her smile turned to a frown of dismay when no male voices greeted her. A quick search indicated that Evan had headed to the beach and Jacob had accompanied him.

As she swapped her shoes for a pair of beach flats, her mood elevated again. A rush of happiness spread through her at her son's decision to swim. He seemed to be gaining confidence and self-assurance, and she attributed both to Jacob's excellent influence.

Jacob was responsible and caring, intent on building a careful and considerate rapport with Evan. He clearly enjoyed the boy's company, communicating and focusing on him.

She closed the distance on the short path to Pelican Beach, following sandy footprints. She paused and shaded her eyes. Head down, Jacob stood talking on his cell phone.

Her gaze riveted on Evan poised at the top of a rocky ledge.

A wave of icy, stark fear flowed through her, and her blood froze.

Her son was a good swimmer. But—

Without warning, Evan lost his balance on the rocks.

"Evan, be careful!" She trembled. Her pulse skittered.

He righted himself and stretched out his arms.

Unease spun up her spine. She broke into a run at the sight of him diving into the water and heard herself scream. A lead weight took up residence in her stomach.

From her peripheral vision, she noticed Jacob. He'd clicked off his cell phone and stood motionless for a split-second. His failure to act didn't escape her.

"Jacob!" She caught up with him and grabbed his arm as he lunged toward the water with her. "What are you waiting for?"

A roll of waves washed up to the shore, as Evan broke the water's surface.

Penelope reached him first. "Have you lost all your common sense?" Her speech was mumbled, echoing in her ears. Her mouth was dry.

Evan's wet swimming trunks were plastered to his legs. He was drenched.

"Don't have a fit, Mom. I didn't fall in if that's what you're upset about."

Despite the coolness in the air, she was sweating. "Think about how high the ledge is. What you did was nothing short of reckless." She glared at Jacob as she wrenched a towel from him. Her hands shook as she wrapped the towel around her shivering son.

The threesome returned to the houseboat without speaking, their footfalls heavy in the sand. Evan pleaded tiredness, grabbed a protein bar from the kitchen, and headed to his bedroom.

Jacob walked with her to the living room.

"Wanna talk about this?" He crossed his arms, his hip perched on the side of the sofa.

Still fuming, she snapped, "No!"

"Okay. I understand." He gazed at her, waiting several seconds. "Are you certain?"

"More than certain."

"Right. Sure." Soundlessly, he strode from the room.

She stood alone. After a few minutes, her breathing returned to normal, and she no longer gasped.

"Penelope?" Jacob's voice was elevated enough to carry from his bedroom before he reappeared in the living room.

"What?" In the charged silence, she jumped at her name being called.

"I'm leaving." His duffle bag was slung over his shoulder. He unlatched the door leading to the outside walkway.

She regarded him. "You're leaving." They both knew she wasn't asking. She was telling.

"My decision is for the best." He paused, opened the door wider, then turned to watch her.

Her heart thumped louder in her chest. She imagined he might seek forgiveness for his negligence and beg her to let him stay. But he didn't assume any wrongness for allowing her son to attempt such a dangerous stunt. He didn't speak or beg. He said nothing.

"I assumed you were here until Sunday," she finally spoke.

"No reason to extend my holiday."

"Because of what happened at the beach?" She flinched at the renewed remembrance, and the terrible dreamlike pang in her chest when she'd viewed Evan's wild dive into the sea.

Jacob shrugged. "That's part of it. But I'll never be able to get through to you."

"Evan could have drowned."

"He didn't drown. He's safe. He's an excellent swimmer and he chose to dive in. He's old enough to determine his strengths and skills."

She pushed out a breath. Jacob was a doctor, a pediatrician, and worked with children. But he didn't have any children of his own.

"You should've stopped him when he started climbing the ledge," she said.

"I wanted to allow Evan some freedom. He's a fearless kid. That's a good thing."

Goosebumps traveled up her arms at the thought of what could have happened. "Is it?"

"Yes." Jacob turned on his heel and swung toward the door.

"Fearlessness doesn't keep him from danger." She lashed out at Jacob's retreating back. "You're not a parent. You could never understand."

He twisted. His dark-brown eyes flared with emotion. "This conversation isn't only about Evan. It concerns you. You're sheltering him too much and he can't be wrapped in cotton forever. What are you afraid of?"

She cringed. Jacob's remarks hit home, but she refused to admit he was right. "You don't know my whole story."

"I know enough. I know about your divorce and your move back to Roses. I know you hate your job and—"

How could she explain her childhood and her domineering father? And her loneliness after Roy's infidelity? Or her sadness and impending dread at spending the Christmas holiday alone—without a loving partner to share each special moment? She'd sound pathetic and needy, a side of her she refused to expose. He knew enough about her already.

She supported herself by leaning against the wall. She attempted to compose her features, though she was crying.

"Hey, beautiful." He stepped toward her, his expression softening. "You're carrying too much on your shoulders. You're a single mother and work too hard."

He offered consolation, though she refused to accept. She didn't need his pity. She was a competent woman who had learned to rely on herself.

"When Evan was young, he was afraid of heights." A tear trickled down her cheek. "Ironic, isn't it?"

Jacob caught her rebellious tear with his forefinger. Gentleness filled his eyes. "He overcame his fear."

"He was overly cautious. I was mindful and tried to encourage him."

"You obviously did a good job."

She inhaled and stepped back, eyeing the open doorway. The sun was beginning to set, and its fiery golden glow lit the harbor. Several boat lights flashed. A seagull perched on one leg on the handrail of the roped walkway. The bird seemed undecided whether to dive into the water or fly away.

"Evan is all I have," she said quietly.

"You have me."

She let out a sob as the bird flew up into the sky. "Do I?"

His gaze never left her face. "I'm here, aren't I?"

She took in his handsome features, those soulful eyes, and his firm, chiseled mouth. He was the epitome of maleness, and all she'd dreamed about since they'd met.

But then another thought forced its way in. She couldn't endure any more heartbreak.

Jacob moved forward. She moved backward. The gap between them stretched a few feet, though figuratively the distance could be measured in miles.

"Evan is a smart, intuitive kid," Jacob said. "He recognizes even more about you than I do."

"Like what?"

"He realizes you've never gotten over your divorce and your ex's betrayal. Evan worries about you because you worry about him. And too much worry isn't good for a kid."

"What you're saying isn't logical."

"Think about it, Penelope. I'm perfectly logical." The edge in Jacob's tone caused her defenses to rise. "And there's something else that drives me bloody insane."

"What?"

"I get that your marriage ended unhappily, and you felt betrayed." He stiffened; his entire body strained in an unbending line. "But why won't you give us a chance?"

"You're spouting opinions as if you were a psychologist." Words caught in her throat. "You're a pediatrician, Jacob."

Oh, but he was right. He'd scored a bullseye. She didn't allow any man to get too close.

"Why are you so frightened of a second opportunity for happiness?" he asked.

Why? Maybe because she was afraid her intense love for him might consume her. If something happened ... if he broke her heart, he'd break Evan's heart, too. And Evan was too vulnerable.

"I appreciate your concern, but I'm well, and so is Evan." Her tone raised and her eyes smarted with tears she refused to shed. "Safe travels, and please don't try to contact me."

He paused, unmoving, forcing her to stare into his fathomless eyes. This wasn't the moment to remember his tender kisses, the upcoming festive celebrations she'd anticipated sharing with him. A happy Christmas, brimming with gladness and miracles.

He fished in his duffle bag and pulled out a gift, meticulously wrapped in red and green foil paper, and handed the package to her.

"I planned to give you this tomorrow. I envisioned us sitting under the tree with mugs of soup. Well, I'm some kind of fool, aren't I?" The sharp tone of his voice was tempered, though his words were weighty and significant. "In any event, Penelope, Merry Christmas."

CHAPTER 12

$\mathcal{B}$ack in Roses on the Monday after Thanksgiving, Penelope found that she could hardly concentrate. Although Jacob texted often, her replies were short.

Can we talk? he asked.

Nothing to say, she replied.

I'm sorry about what happened at the beach. I panicked. No excuses. I shouldn't have hesitated.

Apology accepted.

Wanna take a trip to Stone Mountain in Georgia? he inquired the following day. *I'll ask Dr. Hannaway to fill in for me. You and Evan will love it. There are millions of dazzling holiday lights and spectacular shows.*

Sounds like you're reading a pamphlet about the place.

LOL. I am.

No, thank you.

Are you busy?

Always.

What about the Christmas town you mentioned that's about thirty minutes away from Roses?

I can't, she responded.

137

He reverted to: *Can we talk?*

Nothing to say, she repeated.

Have dinner with me. You choose the restaurant.

Her fingers hovered over the phone's keyboard. She wanted to accept his invitation.

But no, she couldn't.

Not possible, she typed. *Please. Leave me alone.*

When one week turned to two, then three, and the calendar dutifully inched closer to Christmas, she came to terms with a cold, hard fact.

After several days of similar texts, Jacob had stopped contacting her. Since then, she hadn't heard a word from him. She drew her arms close to her body and stared down at her empty hands. Good. He was finally doing what she asked.

Then why did her chest ache, and why did she need to gulp air at every turn?

She cried herself to sleep at night and awoke to red eyes and a splotchy face.

When she casually inquired about Jacob after Evan's volunteering sessions at the clinic, Evan ran a hand through his shaggy hair, then tilted his head to study the ceiling, as if to deter her from asking any more questions.

Shanice phoned and confided that Evan had told her that his mother had fallen in love with Jacob, and then she'd sent Jacob packing after a big argument.

"Mom pretends she isn't interested in Dr. Williams," Evan stated. "Though it's obvious, she cares about him a lot." He also added that their disagreement was all his fault.

"Oh, no." Penelope gasped and denied, while a cold weight settled on her chest. "Evan made a reckless choice, but the argument wasn't because of him."

Or was it?

"Evan hasn't told you the entire story," she continued.

"Do tell," Shanice said.

"I left my son in Jacob's care, and Jacob was negligent." Penelope's voice thickened. "However, Jacob did apologize. Several times, in fact."

"Then all is well."

Yet there was more to the story. Penelope's every thought was of Jacob, and, because of her decision to end their relationship, she was forced to shoulder her hurt alone. Perhaps she should have asked him to stay on the houseboat and talk things out as he'd requested. Perhaps she should have answered his texts differently.

He should have persisted.

However, he was too much of a gentleman. He'd listened to her and eventually heeded her instructions. She wondered how long it would take for a handsome, eligible doctor to find someone new—just in time to celebrate the holidays.

Tears trickled down her cheeks, and she furiously brushed them away.

With inner regret, she recognized that Jacob was everything a man should be. He was intelligent, he made her laugh, he was ambitious, and supportive of her business and hobbies. He was dependable, and equally important, an excellent role model for Evan.

Though now he was no longer in her life because she'd pushed him out.

Seasons had changed for her once again, and slowly, her spinning world began to slow down. When she looked around, she realized she was blessed.

Through renewed determination, she threw herself into wood carving, and finished a dozen delightful dolls for Christmas. The dolls were unique, endearing, and no two were the same. The craft kept her mind and hands occupied, and she was grateful for the distraction.

She donated the dolls to the homeless shelter, and Evan brought several to the clinic.

Her toy shop was frenetic with activity, and whenever Penelope lent a hand during a shift, she couldn't help but compare the atmosphere in the shop to a jubilant party. Children were excited. Parents were thrilled. Everyone was kinder at Christmas.

She was busy beyond words.

And she was heartbroken.

Occasionally, Evan mentioned Jacob. She tried to act nonchalant, though her insides cracked. She avoided driving by Jacob's office or the clinic, fearful of encountering him. She never saw him anywhere.

Several days before Christmas, she paused in her kitchen and opened the window, allowing a light winter breeze to freshen the room. December brought unusually warm temperatures to the Carolinas, and, according to the forecast, the prospect of snow grew less promising by the day. Instead, the weather proved mild and wet.

She stood by her granite countertop, sorting two dozen frozen Christmas cookies. True to her word, Meredith Sinclair's daughter had given an invitation to Evan, and Penelope was invited to a cookie exchange on Sunday.

She pondered how to gracefully decline. The toy stores were demanding, but on Sunday every shop was closed, a decision she and Lincoln had made years ago. They gave their employees a break from the workweek to rest and worship God as they chose.

Her mind returned to the cookie exchange. The prospect of conversing with all the other mothers from Evan's class was awkward. They were an elite clique, and she didn't have much in common with them.

Except for one important point. They all had kids the same age and were struggling with the onset of their children's difficult adolescences.

. . .

140

"LET'S GO CHRISTMAS SHOPPING!" Candee phoned Penelope on a gloomy morning a couple of days later. "I'm looking for another gift to put under the tree for my son, preferably something with horses, and it finally stopped raining. Come with me. No excuses allowed."

Penelope cupped her cell phone to her ear. "I'm working at home today and drowning in paperwork."

"Take a lunch break. I insist. I'll pick you up at noon."

Quickly, Penelope changed her sweat suit for tailored black slacks and a green embroidered *Merry Christmas* sweater. She topped the outfit with a woolen coat in a light tan. She cast a quick appraisal of herself in the mirror and pulled her hair back at the crown, allowing a spring of curls to cascade around her face.

At precisely noon, Candee arrived. Candee welcomed the holidays and dressed appropriately in white slacks and a heavy knit red sweater.

"Nothing compares to the thrill of seeing Roses decorated for Christmas," she announced, when Penelope slid into the passenger seat of her car. "The tree in the square is gorgeous at night when it's lit up."

"I read online that the town is encouraging white lights for all the shops, to keep an old-fashioned holiday look," Penelope replied.

"Read? Haven't you seen any of the displays?"

"Not yet." Penelope batted a hand through the air. Her chest tightened around the ever-present heaviness. "The holidays aren't the same for me anymore."

"Make this a magical Christmas. You're the one in control." Candee's tone was confident, though her gaze was anxious as she scanned Penelope's features. "You look pale. Retail therapy will cheer you up."

"My shopping is done. Evan has everything a boy his age needs. Besides, he hardly ever asks for anything."

Except a puppy.

A few minutes later, Candee parked her car, and the two women jostled through the crowds and headed down the main street arm in arm.

Penelope sniffed a temptingly decadent aroma of dark chocolate, along with roasting chestnuts from a sidewalk vendor. The streets hummed with excitement, and Christmas was in the air. Each shop hung wreaths on their front windows, embellished with red and white ticking stripe ribbons. Several vintage wooden sleds stood propped by the doors. The women paused to admire bundles of fragrant garland adorning a clothing boutique's green window boxes.

A smart, fancy French poodle trotted alongside its owner. The poodle's curly-black coat was groomed in the traditional poodle style.

"Dogs are precious." Candee stopped to compliment the dog, then curved to Penelope. "Are you still adopting a puppy from the shelter for Evan?"

"Definitely. The terrier mix had her puppies, and one will be a surprise Christmas gift for Evan." Penelope brightened. "I've checked on the puppies often, and they're all so lovable. Their fur is mostly white, and they have the cutest expressive eyes and ears. Four puppies are still available from the litter and the shelter told me that Evan can choose his favorite."

"When is he flying to Florida?"

"As soon as school lets out. He'll return home on the morning of Christmas Eve."

"His visit is short," Candee said.

"I'll drive him to the airport. He's flying direct, and this is the first time he'll be alone."

"He'll be fine."

Penelope regarded her friend with a level look. "You sound exactly like Jacob."

The women ducked into a candy store, weaved through a

knot of people, and selected slabs of milk chocolate fudge. They claimed two wooden rocking chairs on the store's wide front porch, and remarked on the shoppers as they passed.

Candee bit into a piece of fudge, leaned back in her chair, and closed her eyes. "Heavenly," she moaned. "Now, speaking of Jacob …"

Penelope's stomach lurched. In the weeks since she'd last seen him, she'd considered texting him. Then she wondered why he'd stopped texting her.

She longed to share the incident on Hilton Head Island with her friend. Yet, she was hesitant to burden Candee with her problems.

"When is the last time you saw Jacob?" Candee asked.

"Thanksgiving weekend."

Exactly three weeks, four days, and twenty hours ago, Penelope thought. Not that she was keeping track, of course.

"Jacob bought the dilapidated house on Brook Street that you looked at together. He was able to snag the house for a steal."

"He did?" Infuriated because he hadn't texted to inform her, Penelope sat straighter and placed the fudge on her lap. "When is the closing?"

"The beginning of January. The house needs a tremendous amount of elbow grease, but he is thrilled and intends to set up his physician's practice there."

Penelope's next reaction was an inward burst of pride. Hurray for Jacob for pursuing his dreams. Nonetheless, he hadn't reached out to tell her the exciting news. And she'd been the person who had first showed him the house.

"He asked about you." Candee's quiet voice checked Penelope's thoughts.

"Oh?" Penelope felt her forehead knit into a frown. "What did he say?"

"He said he missed you. Very much."

Penelope shot up from the chair. Her fudge fell from her lap. "Not enough to phone me, though."

"If my opinion will make it easier to admit your feelings for him ..."

Feelings? The fact that she couldn't stop thinking about him? The fact she often played out their argument in her mind, and wished things had turned out differently?

Penelope picked up the fudge, threw it in the trash, and sat back down. How did a woman recover from a broken heart?

You're a professional and selfless woman and absolutely amazing, he had said.

You are beautiful.

No more thinking about him, she scolded herself, yet the memory of his attentiveness, his tender kisses, his kindness, lay suspended in the air.

"Knock, knock, my friend. Come back." Candee reached over and tapped Penelope's shoulder. "That man genuinely cares about you, and I believe you care equally for him. His feelings for you are so intense, it would astonish him if he stopped to examine them. Whatever your differences, please give him a chance."

"He was wrong. He needs to reach out to me again."

"Forgiveness is a powerful gift, especially at Christmas. Accept this gift, for it promises peace. Isn't the holiday all about reconciliation and good will toward men?"

Piped in music from the candy store spilled onto the porch, lyrics of "Tidings of comfort and joy, comfort and joy, oh, tidings of comfort and joy."

"God Rest Ye Merry, Gentlemen." Penelope's beloved Christmas carol. She rocked on the chair as optimism bloomed. Perhaps there was a chance for her and Jacob, after all.

Candee finished her fudge, and the women continued

perusing the shops. Candee spotted an oil painting of a horse for her son's room, while Penelope skirted into a local hardware store.

"Are you handy with tools?" she'd questioned Jacob after they viewed the dilapidated house.

"I don't even own a tool kit," he'd replied.

She didn't understand why she considered buying him a Christmas gift and couldn't imagine when she might give it to him. Nonetheless, she purchased a kit featuring pliers, a hammer, and a screwdriver. It was a start at reconciliation, although later she would wonder what madness had possessed her to buy such a thing, especially when she requested the merchant to wrap the gift in winter wonderland foil paper.

"Did you need some tools?" Candee inquired with a laugh when the women met outside their respective shops. Her gentle prodding made Penelope feel churlish for questioning her purchase. Jacob's smile warmed her heart, and his thoughtfulness toward the community knew no bounds. He was level-headed and tuned into her emotions. Plus, he respected the boundaries she'd set. She couldn't fault him for that.

On the houseboat, he'd looked breathlessly handsome in casual jeans, and his polo shirt had fit his broad shoulders to perfection. She well remembered the thrill of gazing into his dark eyes when they'd captured and held hers.

"I promise," he'd replied when she'd asked him to never turn into her ex, and tenderness had swelled in her heart at his earnest response.

He'd sealed his words with a deep, toe-curling kiss that had left her breathless.

She wasn't certain he loved her, but he did care for her. And after all, it was Christmas. She'd write out a card and congratulate him on his home purchase, then send the gift to the clinic with Evan. She smiled, imagining Jacob unwrapping the gift and then texting her.

She clutched his gift close and strolled the sidewalk with Candee. She flashed her friend a smile when she kept inquiring about Penelope's "secret" from the hardware store, because Penelope refused to divulge the details. Some things, she decided, required a privacy of the heart.

A jarring note of laughter echoed from the steps of a nearby shop. Meredith Sinclair stood with a group of women, her stunning blond hair and slim figure reminding Penelope of a runway model.

"Dr. Williams is coming over for dinner soon," she told the women. "I didn't want the poor man to be alone during the holidays. I'm making my famous baked ham with pineapple and all the trimmings."

"Did he accept?" one of the women asked.

"He said it all depends on his work schedule, but he seemed more than a little interested." With a twitch of her checkered pencil skirt, she reminded that she'd see them all at her cookie exchange on Sunday.

Jacob's social life is none of my business, Penelope thought. She rubbed her forehead and closed her eyes. He was free to date whomever he chose. Besides, she shouldn't have been eavesdropping, though Meredith had spoken loud enough for the entire town to hear.

Penelope had listened to the conversation with annoyed sadness, wondering if Jacob would accept the woman's invitation. In that instant, Penelope resented the town, and all the women's gazes who now seemed focused solely on her.

Her thoughts scrambled. Perhaps she should return to Hilton Head with Evan and live peacefully on the houseboat.

With a look of feigned naiveness, Meredith sidled over. "Penelope, I didn't see you at first. Are you free to attend my cookie exchange on Sunday?"

While Candee looked on, Penelope met Meredith's gaze with measured composure. She took a brief mental pause and focused on the positive things in her life. She'd created an uncluttered, relaxing atmosphere at home. She and Evan were eating healthier, and she was looking forward to spending Christmas Eve with Evan and his new puppy. She was better than jealousy or ill will.

She straightened her shoulders. "Evan is leaving for Florida soon, and we'll be attending to last-minute details," she replied. "I'll donate my cookies to the first responders in town. Thank you for the invite, and I wish you and your family a Merry Christmas."

CHAPTER 13

.

a couple of days later, Penelope found her son in his bedroom, a half-empty, open suitcase on his bed. His phone was propped beside him, tuned to a pop station playing a rock version of "Jingle Bells."

"You haven't finished packing for your trip yet?" she asked.

"Florida is hot, and I won't need much."

"We leave in an hour," Penelope reminded, handing Evan a box wrapped in pink and white paper. "Please give this gift to your father and stepmother for the new baby. I carved a wooden doll for Christina."

"That was nice, Mom. She can't play with it yet."

"Someday." Penelope leaned over and smoothed Evan's dark hair. He sat on the bed with his legs stretched out. Lately, he'd been swimming at the rec center, perfecting his butterfly stroke, and training with the swim coach. He and Zack hung out after school, and Evan looked calmer and happier. He was coming into his own and finding his way.

He scanned her features. "I'll miss you, Mom."

"I'll miss you, too." She regarded her fine-looking son,

and her heart burst with pride. She reached out and gave him a quick hug, envisioning his thrill at the surprise puppy waiting for him when he returned.

"Dr. Williams is working overtime at the clinic." Evan adjusted the volume on his cell phone and the music muted. "You should see his Santa Claus costume. It's too big, and he holds up the pants with a wide black belt. He couldn't find a white beard, but he wears a red velvet hat. Everyone thinks he looks funny. Dr. Hannaway is always serious, but even she laughed when she saw him."

Penelope nodded. "I bet."

"He liked the Christmas cookies you sent, especially the ones with the chocolate filling. He snuck a few while I gave them out to the kids and he said you're an excellent baker. He's working eighteen hours every day between his private practice and the clinic."

They sat in silence for a minute, listening to the next selection on his phone.

"Silent Night." A quiet, peaceful song. Simple.

I'm learning that simple is best, Jacob had mentioned.

"What are we doing on Christmas Eve?" Evan asked. "Uncle Lincoln and Aunt Shanice aren't here."

"I'll pick you up at the airport and in the afternoon, we'll attend church service."

"What will you do when I'm in Florida with Dad?"

"There is plenty of work at the toy shop to keep me busy. Don't worry."

Evan worries about you because you worry about him, Jacob had said. *And too much worry isn't good for a kid.*

She squeezed Evan's hand. "I love you, and you've made me infinitely proud. When your father and I divorced, I was stuck, but you're here, we're together, and I'm happy it's Christmas."

"Okay, Mom, okay." His smile was affectionate. "Can I tell you something?"

"Of course."

He darted a glance at her and took a deep breath. "Remember when Zack's mother got into an accident?"

Her heart stilled. "How could I forget?"

"I told you she backed into a mailbox near the rec center."

"Right."

"I have a confession." He pulled at the collar of his T-shirt and shifted on the bed. "I lied to you, and I'm sorry. After we stopped for milk shakes that day, I asked Zack's mother to drive us to the animal shelter to see the dogs. I didn't want to get you upset and tell you. I knew we were already late, but I couldn't resist."

"You're forgiven for lying." Penelope fought against the impulse to reprimand him. Lecturing wasn't helpful, and she understood his underlying reason. "I love dogs, too."

"So does Dr. Williams."

Her emotions swung back and forth between desire and despondency at the mention of Jacob's name.

"If you're geared to homeschool next semester, we can live on Hilton Head Island," she offered.

"Are you kidding? I'm trying out for the swim team, and we practice every day after school." Evan drew his legs up and rested his chin on his knees. "Someday, when I go to college, I'd like to study abroad. Maybe I'll win a scholarship. My coach said there are loads of opportunities if I practice real hard."

The idea of Evan leaving and going to another country brought tears to her eyes and a discreet sniff she hoped he didn't hear.

"Not forever," Evan assured. "I'll come back often. I promise. Especially for Christmas."

"All kids should travel abroad." Her voice broke as she

pulled him into another hug. "Your experiences there will frame the rest of your life."

"You're a cool mother," Evan said. "Now I need to finish packing."

AFTER PENELOPE DROPPED Evan off at the airport with a tearful goodbye, she hurried home. Obsessing over the details, she'd set up a puppy checklist and purchased water bowls, a crate, puppy food, a dog bed, toys, and a leash. She'd hid all the items in the garage.

Satisfied the house was prepped and ready for the precious, cute addition, the next few days passed quickly. Evan texted when he'd landed in Florida. He assured he was having a good time and that baby Christina was adorable, although she cried a lot.

Occasionally, when Penelope passed the decorated Christmas tree in the living room, she glanced under it. Several bundled packages topped with gold ribbon were from Lincoln and Shanice, plus an assortment of gifts from her ex that he'd sent ahead for Evan.

Jacob's tool kit sat wrapped in the winter wonderland paper, and she pondered when she'd ever give it to him. Alongside was the gift he'd given her, packaged in red and green paper. She hadn't opened his gift. Obviously, he hadn't opened hers.

The realization made her want to pour out her sorrow, the pang of longing so strong, she felt weak. She wrapped her arms around her stomach and hunched over, overcome with sadness. Jacob was so impressive, so kind, so remarkably good-looking. If he'd only text her again, she'd agree to see him.

No, no. She couldn't waste her emotions on a man who didn't care. She deserved more from him. And he deserved more from her. Regardless, they couldn't give each other what they both needed because pride stood in the way.

Lincoln phoned and requested she fly to Virginia to tidy up loose ends from the recent acquisition. Though reluctant, she asked pointed questions and eventually agreed. Dismissing her negative thoughts, she pushed up the sleeves of her wool blazer and flew the short, round trip to Virginia the following day.

As PLANNED, Penelope picked Evan up at the airport on Christmas Eve day.

They stopped home to change and unpack. Mindful they were picking up his puppy after the afternoon church service, she dressed in gray slacks and a silvery sweater adorned with snowflakes. Lately, her clothes fit better, and she attributed her success to healthier eating. She had also initiated an exercise routine, which included a thirty-minute daily walk.

A Scottish plaid scarf, red quilted vest, and high leather boots completed her ensemble. Tasteful, yet casual enough to handle a wriggling puppy.

She paused to study her reflection in the hallway mirror before they left for church. When she tucked an errant tendril behind her ear, her faux diamond stud earrings flashed back at her. She'd styled her hair in a loose bun, adorned with a pearl clip.

Evan wore tan-colored chinos, a polo shirt, and his black leather jacket.

The rain had cleared out, and the forecast had changed. There was a possibility of snow for Christmas Day, the weatherman declared, which was a huge event for the Southern residents of Roses.

After pausing to speak with the pastor and admire the

live nativity after church, she drove to the animal shelter as early evening neared. A star-spangled sky promised clear weather, at least for now.

She'd checked ahead to be certain the shelter was open, and the volunteer assured two puppies were available for adoption.

"Mom, this isn't the way to our house," Evan reminded.

Hardly able to contain her excitement, she parked in front of the shelter. The interior lights blazed, cordial and welcoming.

She swallowed a laugh. "Are you ready to take your new puppy home?"

His eyes rounded. He clutched the door handle, then swiveled to her, his face beaming with elation. "You mean it?"

"Absolutely." She embraced him, envisioning his joy at seeing the puppies. "Merry Christmas!"

He burst into tears. "Don't mind me, Mom." He wiped his wet cheeks with a chagrined smile. "I'm just so happy."

A car pulled up and parked behind them. She stole a glance in the rearview mirror, and her hand went to her throat. A very yellow, very recognizable Volkswagen.

"Yay, it's Santa Claus." Evan threw a fist pump, then flung open the door and dashed from the truck.

Penelope got out and leaned against her truck. Her heart raced.

A tall, broad-shouldered man, carrying a bouquet of roses, strode toward her. A whisper of moonlight lit his path.

And he wasn't Santa.

"Hi, Evan." Jacob pulled off his red velvet hat and shoved it in the pocket of his rumpled Santa suit. "Hello, Penelope."

"Jacob." Incredulous, Penelope hung back in surprise. She searched for her voice and couldn't find it. "Are you here for a puppy?"

"I'm here for you, Penelope." He laid the bouquet on the hood of the truck. "Merry Christmas."

Breathe, Penelope, breathe. The fragrant scent of a dozen red roses wafted in the night air. "You're not working at the clinic?"

"I've seen patients all day. Dr. Hannaway stepped in for me."

"Mom is getting me a puppy, Dr. Williams!" Evan's eyes sparkled.

She gave Evan a radiant smile and nodded toward the animal shelter. "The volunteer is waiting for you. There are two puppies left to be adopted."

Evan broke into a run and took the stairs to the shelter three at a time. With a decided wave, he hurried inside.

"I'll meet you in a minute," she called out to him.

Jacob's posture was still. He released a sigh and stared at her. "Penelope, you are amazing."

"I planned this ahead."

"You're a planner."

He resembled a man who had just stepped out of her favorite romance novel, a handsome hero, though he had a full day's growth of a dark beard. He looked thinner, yet perhaps she imagined it.

"Why are you here?" Her voice shook.

"You ignored me. I waited like you asked, but when I didn't hear from you, I resorted to Plan B."

A thought niggled, then broke free. He'd done the gentlemanly thing, abiding by her wishes. And then he hadn't.

Curious, she tilted her head up. "What is Plan B?"

"It's my twofold puppy plan. Evan and I volunteered at the shelter, and I got friendly with everyone." His deep voice strengthened. "Sure enough, they mentioned you planned to surprise Evan on Christmas Eve."

He stepped forward. Curtains stirred in the windows of

nearby residents. Twinkling white lights shone from inside. The smell of wood-burning fireplaces permeated the air.

She gestured toward the homes. "There's the disadvantage of small-town living. Everyone knows everybody else's business."

"The advantages are a close-knit community and slower pace." Jacob's lips curved into a smile. "Oh, let's see, and a quaint, idyllic community, and a beautiful woman. A woman I'd really like to date again."

Tears swelled in her eyes. "You're working nonstop."

"I'm changing my schedule. Along with several other aspects of my life."

"You bought the house we looked at. Candee told me."

He chuckled. "A cheap house will allow me to work less, plus I'll be able to have an office there and see patients. The home is a start, but I need more."

"What do you need?"

"You." He caught a stray tear that trickled down her cheek. "Even though you broke my heart."

She inhaled, drawing a sharp breath. "I did? I didn't realize—"

"That I loved you? Well, I do. And I apologize for what happened at Pelican Beach. If you give me a second chance to prove myself ..." He quirked an eyebrow and smiled. "After all, it is Christmas."

"Jacob, please don't apologize. You did nothing wrong. You care. That's not a fault."

The chemistry between them crackled. There was magic in the air. The magic that came with Christmas. The magic that came with love.

Her anger at him had been foolish and juvenile. She'd lashed out at him, though Roy had been the source of her hurt and insecurities.

"My mum and sister are moving back to Melbourne," Jacob said. "I told them I'd visit."

"Good."

"Will you join me? With Evan?" His words rushed together. "You can talk to me nonstop on the plane. I realize flying is involved unless—"

"Jacob, I ... I need a second ... I wanted to tell you I flew to Virginia recently." She dragged air into her lungs. "I was afraid at first, but then I realized there was something else I was even more afraid of than flying."

He gathered her in his arms and drew her close. Nearer, tighter. "What?"

She pressed a hand to his heart. "I was afraid I had lost you because I pushed you away. I love you, too."

"You'll never lose me. Roses is where I intend to stay." He traced her lips with his fingers. "Will you give me another chance?"

"I have a son."

"An amazing son. As amazing as his mother."

She ran her fingers along his strong cheekbones. She loved his good-looking features, his nearness, his solid hold. She turned her face into his chest and listened to the steady thud of his heart.

He lifted her chin and cupped her face in his hands. He kissed her, slowly at first, warm and emotional, then more intensely as his mouth captured hers. "I love you, Penelope. You're special, and when I lost you from my life, I knew I needed to find a way to bring us together."

She grinned. "Plan B?"

"The twofold puppy plan."

"Wait." Her grin widened. "What do you mean by twofold?"

A shout from the shelter's entrance startled her, and she pulled back from Jacob's embrace.

"Mom, are you coming inside?" Evan cuddled two fluffy, cream-colored puppies in his arms. "I chose my puppies!"

She shuffled back a step. "Puppies? As in, more than one?"

"They're brother and sister. They can't be separated because I named them." Evan's face was flushed and radiant. "Come and meet Kris and Kringle. Kris is the boy and Kringle is the girl. You'll fall in love. I promise."

"We're already in love," Jacob whispered. He twined his fingers around hers and led her toward the entrance.

"All this love at Christmas." She smiled and affectionately nudged him. She was at ease with her world.

"Doctor Williams, your dog is waiting for you," Evan declared as they approached.

Penelope touched her throat. Her breath stalled. "Jacob, you're adopting a dog, too?"

"Truth?" He grinned and kissed her temple.

"Uh-huh."

"I'm adopting Nutcracker." His dark eyes lit with an inner glow. "What better way to celebrate Christmas than with two puppies, a mother dog, a stepson, and a beautiful wife?"

"Stepson? And wife?"

"A fantastic stepson and a *beautiful* wife. Penelope Reid, will you marry me?"

She answered without hesitation. Her smile filled with love as she rested her trembling hand on his cheek. "My answer is yes. Yes, yes."

EPILOGUE

*ne Year Later*

"WHO EATS quinoa and red peppers during the holidays?" Evan asked.

"We do." Penelope held up her *Change Your Holiday Menu, Change Your Life* cookbook. "Don't you want to continue to eat healthy?"

"This year I vote for cream cheese cookies." Evan looked to Jacob for backup.

Jacob chuckled and raised his hand. "I second the cookie vote."

His wife stood at the stainless-steel sink. The sink at his new house on Brook Street, Jacob thought with a satisfied smile.

Penelope drummed her fingers on the counter and grinned at them both. "Don't either of you like quinoa?"

"I tried it last year," Jacob replied.

"And?"

"I agree with my stepson. Cookies are better." Jacob strode to her and wrapped his arms around her waist. Strains of "It's Beginning to Look a Lot Like Christmas" wafted from the living room stereo.

She gazed at him over her shoulder. "I'm not baking any more cookies, because we're flying to Australia in a few days."

He pressed a kiss on her fragrant hair. Today, she held it back with a silver spangled clip.

"Fortunately, you froze two bags of your chocolate cream cheese cookies in November," he said. "They're my favorite."

She pulled from his embrace, stepped to the refrigerator, and rummaged in the freezer. "Then why is there only one bag of cookies left?"

Jacob and Evan pointed at each other, winked conspiratorially, then burst out laughing. "Recently, we had a late-night cookie festival," Jacob confessed.

She laughed, revealing her adorable dimples. She was gorgeous when she laughed. Her eyes were soft and shiny.

"I'm outnumbered by animals in this house." She gazed at the two sleeping dogs in the corner: Kris and Kringle. They weren't considered puppies anymore, though Kris still had puppy energy, and Kringle continued to chew on everything in sight. True to their breed, the dogs were willful, independent, and more than a little stubborn. However, they'd settled into the routine of life at the Williams' new home.

"What do Australians eat at Christmas, Dad?" Evan swiped three cookies from the freezer bag and placed them in the microwave to thaw.

Dad. Jacob took the word to heart. His stepson's acceptance and love meant the world.

"We usually begin with prawns at lunchtime. Lots and lots of prawns and they are massive. My sister is making lasagna, so at least we'll get our lasagna." Jacob gave a thumbs-up to Evan. "And my mum is serving a cold roasted chicken."

"Why cold?"

"It's too hot in Australia in December to cook a lot. Fortunately, my mum and sister bought a home with a pool, and you'll still be able to keep up with your swim practice."

Penelope caught Jacob's gaze and smiled. "Melbourne. Your hometown."

"Yea. I'm looking forward to showing you and Evan the sights." His chest expanded with each breath. "I remember restaurants by the Yarra River, and my mum is excited about the performing arts complex."

His mum had sold the farm at a profit, and she insisted that he no longer needed to send her money. Along with the savings on the inexpensive home purchase, he'd curtailed his hours at the clinic and hired another doctor. Seeing patients at his home office enabled him to spend more time with Penelope and Evan, the two loves of his life.

Spurred by Penelope's encouragement, Jacob had phoned and spoken with his mum and sister for hours. They'd shared stories about his niece, Linda, and grieved, while continuing to cope with the devastating loss. They sought comfort in their memories and had resolved to stick together.

"Australia is far away." Evan glanced at his two dogs. No longer puppies, Kris and Kringle resembled their mother, with white coats and almond-shaped eyes. Their paws turned out, and the distinctive pink markings they once had on their nose and paws had changed to black. "I'll miss them."

"Uncle Lincoln and Aunt Shanice will take excellent care of our animals," Penelope assured him.

"Nutcracker, Kris, Kringle, and Giblet." Evan grabbed the cookies from the microwave, shouldered his swim bag, and started for the door. "Gotta go. Practice begins in an hour and Zack's mother is picking me up."

"Have fun," Jacob and Penelope chimed.

Once Evan left, Jacob grabbed Penelope's hand and led her to the living room. Nutcracker, never far behind Jacob, took up her favorite spot by the fireplace.

They'd positioned Penelope's faux fir tree by the front window, and decorated it for Christmas in a tasteful, subdued flair. His tool kit sat under the tree. A thoughtful gift. Last year, they'd chuckled with the realization that it would take more than a tool kit to renovate a fixer upper on Jacob's limited budget. Together as a family, they'd painted floorboards, discarded the ancient front door for a new red one, and hung curtains. They'd left carpet, bathrooms, and kitchen appliance installation and remodeling to the professionals.

But renovate they had. Room by room, until the Victorian shone shiny and preserved. Jacob adored the home's character, the quirky light fixtures, and the unique woodwork and intricate moldings.

Penelope elected to place his Christmas gift to her from last year, the photo he'd taken of her when they'd first met at the airport, on the coffee table.

He smiled as he regarded the photo. His beautiful wife, wearing a cream-colored crepe blouse and brown slacks. Her dark hair, shaped in a short bob style, had grown longer this past year. Silver highlights still framed her lovely face.

The photo was placed in a glass frame alongside a stack of romance books. A row of carved wooden dolls, all named for various spices, were ready to be transported to the nearest hospital or shelter for children of all ages to enjoy.

After Penelope and Jacob had wed six months earlier, and his house was finally livable, she and Evan had moved in. Candee had secured a buyer for Penelope's house the first day she'd put it on the market. Success all around.

"I'm glad you decided to cut back your hours at the toy shop," he said, pulling her beside him on the sofa.

"Me too, yet the decision was difficult." She offered a tremulous smile that touched his heart. "I love my craft. Woodworking is infinitely rewarding."

"You're amazing and talented, beautiful." He brought her fingers to his lips for a kiss. "Do you know how much I love you?" His heart filled with more emotion than he thought it could hold—happiness, appreciation, and love.

"I hope looking after all our animals isn't asking too much from Lincoln and Shanice," she said. "They were out of town last Christmas—"

"And we'll be out of town this Christmas," Jacob finished.

She gazed up at him. "Are you certain the only flight you were able to book leaves on Christmas Day?"

"Yea. The trip takes about twenty hours, with two stopovers."

She shuddered and threw him an accusing stare. "Crikey."

He laughed. "Just sleep, eat, watch movies, and, most importantly, talk."

"Okay." She sighed and snuggled nearer him.

He gazed around his home. A beaut. His dream for a simple, rewarding life had come true. What a wonderful road he and Penelope had traveled. Eighteen months ago, he'd never have imagined a Christmas like this.

Though here he was, in this Americana town he called home, with a woman he loved more than anything in the world. When he'd surprised her at the animal shelter on Christmas Eve almost a year ago and declared his love, she'd cast aside her pride because she loved him, too. And that remembrance would remain in his heart forever.

He'd changed his lifestyle to accommodate his beliefs and found love in the bargain. Finally, he was at ease with his world.

"Jacob?" Penelope asked.

He gazed into her compelling eyes and outlined the curve of her jaw and cheeks. "Hmm?"

"How will we celebrate Christmas if we're not in Roses, or even in Australia yet?"

"Simple." He drew her close and kissed her. "We'll celebrate Christmas in the air."

THE END

A NOTE FROM JOSIE

Dear Reader,

Thank you for spending the holidays in Roses with Penelope and Jacob.

Christmas in the Air is the sixth book in my contemporary 1-800-series, set in the charming fictional small town of Roses, North Carolina.

What if you told your innermost secrets to a guy you assumed you'd never see again?

With this book, I introduce Dr. Jacob Williams to our beloved mix of familiar heroes and heroines. Jacob is from Australia, and he and Penelope first meet on an airplane bound for Hilton Head Island. Penelope Reid was featured in *1-800-NEW YEAR*, book five of the series. She has relocated to Roses with her son, Evan, who is on the cusp of adolescence.

If this story moved you, please help other readers find it by posting a review.

Christmas in the Air is available in ebook, paperback, large print paperback, audiobook, and hardcover.

I would love to meet you in person someday, but in the

meantime, please accept my sincere and grateful thank you. Without your support, my books would not be possible.

As I write my next sweet romance, I leave you with this: Have you ever held back from a dream because it mattered too much to risk? I did, when I started writing. Take the chance and do what you love.

With sincere appreciation,

Josie Riviera

Love music?

My Spotify Playlist for Christmas in the Air is here.

Want more of the 1-800-Series, Flipping For You?

Click here.

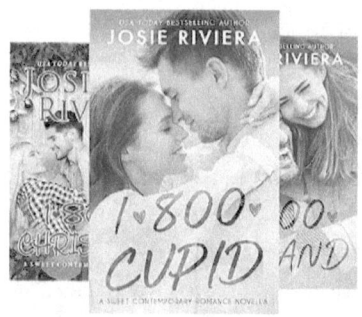

Or grab the 1-800-Series Collection.

The entire series! 6 sweet romances in 1 giant boxed set.

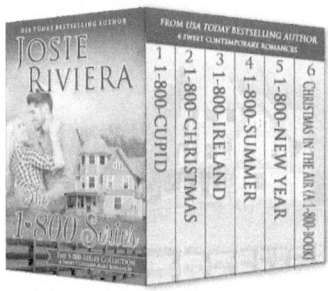

If you can't resist adorable puppies and sweet holiday romance, my Pawfect Christmas Hearts boxed set is here.

The books included in the set are:
A Christmas Puppy to Cherish
Christmas in the Air
Cocoa's Christmas Love
Grab your copy of Pawfect Christmas Hearts today!

5 STAR READER REVIEWS

"Wonderful story!" - Amazon Reviewer

"Great story! The plot flowed well and the characters were realistic.

The story follows two older adults... that, mostly, behave like adults. Their traumas and insecurities played out well. We see the characters overcome them, or at least power through them with less anxiety than they previously had.

The adults bring out the best in each other and it was refreshing to see the near-teen be the first to out that out."- MaryEllen

"A heartwarming story of hope, forgiveness, new beginnings, a HEA, and puppies!"- Amazon Reviewer

And reviews from my other 1-800-series books:

"Author Josie Riviera has once again drawn me into one of her wonderful stories."- Amazon Reviewer

"Josie Riviera writes such great romance stories, whether historical or contemporary, and I knew I had to read this one just from seeing the title of the book. The storyline is a beautifully written clean romance. I enjoy romances where the characters are more mature and relatable. She has created characters with interactions that are believable, cast in a setting described so vividly it made me want to live there!"- Amazon Reviewer

RECIPE FOR TERESA'S CREAM CHEESE CHRISTMAS COOKIES

Ingredients:
   1 3 oz. package of cream cheese
   2 sticks of butter (softened)
   1 cup flour
   Shape into 24 one-inch balls and press into small muffin tins, and then add filling.

There are 3 different fillings:
   Filling One:
   1 egg
   1 tablespoon soft butter
   ¾ cup brown sugar

1 tsp. vanilla
Chopped mixed nuts

Filling Two:
6 oz. cream cheese
½ cup sugar
1 egg with a teaspoon of lemon juice

Filling Three: (chocolate)
6 oz. chocolate chips, melted
Add:
¼ cup sugar
1 tablespoon milk
1 beaten egg
1 teaspoon vanilla
1 tablespoon butter

Mix and half fill each cup with filling of your choice.
Bake at 350 degrees for fifteen minutes.
Enjoy!

BONUS: SNEAK PEEK AT 1-800-CUPID

Chapter One:

Twenty thousand dollars.
Click.

173

Candee Contando licked her dry lips. She'd done it. She'd placed an online bid on a home-auction website for the Victorian mansion on Thompson Lane. Her dream home, her dollhouse. Her dilapidated project.

Two years of savings. Gone.

No matter. Under her guidance, she'd transform the mansion to its former majestic state, painted a mustard-yellow offset by ornamental burnt-sienna "gingerbread" trim. The sounds of children's giggling and music and barking beagles—yes, beagles—would echo across all five acres of the property.

She surveyed her offer and beamed, savoring the moment.

Now if she only could ensure that no one else bid on the property and drove up the price.

She studied the ticking clock on the website. Stay optimistic, she told herself. Deteriorated by age and wear, the Victorian would scare off any prospective buyer.

She pushed away from her desk and surveyed her real estate office. Although only one room, she prided herself on the cheery décor. One wall featured photos of North Carolina—the majestic peaks of the Blue Ridge parkway and scenic waterfalls. Below the photos hung a map of the area with local real estate listings highlighted by pushpins.

She peered out the window into the street below. Since noon, a bright sun had been at odds with January's wind—a wind crazy in its intent to blow the streetlights off their wires.

For the umpteenth time, she checked her nonringing cell phone for messages. Surely the real estate market in Roses, North Carolina, would improve. Didn't prospective home buyers begin looking in January? And wouldn't these buyers call her rather than her competitors? Candee prided herself on her professionalism and up-to-date listings.

Then why hadn't she made a single sale since August?

On the heel of that depressing assessment came a cheerful one. In two hours, she and her older sister, Desiree, planned to enjoy dinner at Desiree's country club.

Candee stepped back to her desk and switched off the computer.

Two single women in their late twenties, she mused, spending Friday night alone and dateless, four weeks before Valentine's Day.

Her cell phone rang, most likely Desiree firming up dinner plans and reminding Candee not to be late. Regardless of what time Candee met her older sister anywhere, Desiree always arrived before her.

Candee clicked on her phone. "1-800-Cupid," she said with a laugh.

"Contando Realty?" a man asked.

"Yes, yes …" So much for professionalism. Candee felt her cheeks color. She hurried to her desk, dropping into the chair and switching her phone to speaker. "Are you looking to buy a home today, sir?"

"I am." The man hesitated. "Is this the correct number?"

She powered on her computer. "Absolutely."

"I'm new to the area and checked into the Roses Hotel last night," he said.

Envisioning the rundown hotel, Candy raised her eyebrows. Although in all fairness, the hotel was the only lodging open in the winter. Roses, North Carolina, was a summer tourist town known for bubbling hot springs and cool mountain temperatures.

Her fingers poised on the keyboard. "I'm more than happy to assist. Your name?"

"Teddy. Teddy Winchester." He had a deep voice, a slight southern drawl.

"What type of home are you searching for, Mr. Winchester?"

"The worst home in the best neighborhood."

Yup. It figured. No significant sales commission to pay the mortgage this month. Fortunately, her part-time job at the local hardware store was stable, although the pay was meager.

She scrolled through the listings. "For yourself, sir?"

"I'm an investor."

"How many bedrooms and baths?"

"Three bedrooms, two baths. Single family and one level."

"Budget?"

"Anything below $50,000."

She rubbed the back of her neck. *Who did he think she was, a miracle worker?*

"Mr. Winchester, the nicer neighborhoods in Roses are priced well above $100,000."

"Nope. Too high."

Certainly a man of few words.

"Perhaps—"

"I'll take another look on the Internet." He seemed to ignore her completely. "Thanks anyway."

She wouldn't lose a potential sale.

"Wait." She feigned checking a non-existent schedule. "I may have an opening this afternoon. I know the area well and I'll find properties to show you. Will three o'clock work?"

"In a half hour? Fine. I admire a realtor who works fast. Should I meet you at your office? The address is listed on the Internet."

Candee verified the street number and ended the phone call with a cheery, "See you at three."

She clicked off and checked her watch. Thirty minutes wasn't enough time to drive to her apartment and change. Her worn jeans and blue flannel shirt would have to suffice.

Immediately, she phoned Desiree. "I may be late for dinner."

"I'm so glad it's you," Desiree said. "Scott, a new lawyer at the firm, asked me out tonight. Barring the fact the invitation was last minute, I said yes. Desperation, right?" She paused. "Can we plan for dinner together tomorrow night instead?"

"Right, sure. The reason I called is because I have a client who's interested in seeing some properties."

"You have a real live client?" Desiree cut immediately to the question.

Candee envisioned her sister, thick blonde hair piled high, sitting behind a mahogany desk in her law firm. Proper, well-dressed, every inch the high-powered attorney. Desiree had proven that, with the right help, a disadvantaged childhood could lead to a successful adulthood. She worked late hours at her law firm advocating justice for low-income families and their children.

"He's an investor," Candee said.

"Maybe he's tall, dark, and handsome?" Desiree said with deceptive casualness. "And rich?"

"Investors are usually short bald men." Candee adjusted her shirt's wrinkled collar, then checked out the frayed hem of her jeans. She let out a frustrated groan and ran a hand through her unruly auburn waves.

"You'll need a rich man if you plan to go through with your insane idea to purchase that Victorian," Desiree said. "The place will eat up all the money you hope to earn in a lifetime."

"I'll handle most of the work myself. Remember, when we lived in foster care, I learned carpentry from the family who took us in."

"How will you offer a quality after-school environment to disadvantaged kids if you're busy driving nails into crumbling walls?"

"Watch me." Briefly, Candee squeezed her eyes shut. It was her turn to pay it forward.

"Well, don't discount short men. They prefer tall, willowy red-heads with green eyes," Desiree said. "Who knows? He might be struck by Cupid's golden arrow when he meets you. This guy might be the one."

Candee drew in a breath. "The one what, exactly?"

"Your partner, your love, your support system. The one who can help pay off the mountainous amount of debt you'll incur if you actually buy the biggest dilapidated disaster in the state."

"Someone supportive? For me? After what happened?"

Desiree's voice grew quieter. "Not every guy pretends to be something he's not."

A lump lodged in Candee's throat. No man was worth having her heart broken again, although she didn't vocalize her feelings. Desiree was an eternal romantic.

With a promise to meet her sister on Saturday evening, Candee clicked off and bent to pick up a broken pencil lying on the floor. Not once since the ill-fated night two years ago when her long-time boyfriend had walked out had she broken the vow to herself and wept. Life went on, although a sadness she couldn't shake remained precariously close to the surface.

Some lessons were more difficult than others. Her ex had taught her the hardest—she wasn't interesting enough, pretty enough or vivacious enough.

Tears welled and she brushed them away. Standing, she tossed the pencil into a garbage can by the door. While she confirmed two house showings for Mr. Winchester, she cast a critical assessment of her reflection in the mirror by the office door. She pinched her pale cheeks and added a touch of rose lip balm to her lips. Then she gathered her hair into a ponytail, securing the thick curls with an elastic band. With a final glance in the mirror, she pulled on her cream-colored woolen jacket and wound an emerald-green paisley scarf around her neck.

Her suede purse under her arm, she pushed open the exit doors and stepped outside. The sun had buried itself under a formless cloud, and a swirl of wind blew her paisley scarf across her face. She tucked it securely beneath the collar of her jacket. The day was typical January weather for Roses, undecided if it was warm or cold.

*** End of Excerpt 1-800-CUPID by Josie Riviera ***

Copyright © 2018 Josie Riviera

Want more? Keep reading *1-800-CUPID.*

FREE on Kindle Unlimited!

ABOUT THE AUTHOR

Josie Riviera is a *USA TODAY* bestselling author of contemporary, inspirational, and historical sweet romances that read like Hallmark movies. She lives in the Charlotte, NC, area with her wonderfully supportive husband. They share their home with an adorable shih tzu, who constantly needs grooming, and live in an old house forever needing renovations.

Become a member of my Read and Review VIP Facebook group for exclusive giveaways and ARCs.

To connect with Josie, visit her webpage and subscribe to her newsletter. As a thank-you, she'll send you a free sweet romance novella directly to your inbox.

josieriviera.com

PRAISE AND AWARDS

USA TODAY bestselling author

ACKNOWLEDGMENTS

An appreciative thank you to my patient husband, Dave, and our three wonderful children.

ALSO BY JOSIE RIVIERA

Seeking Patience
Seeking Catherine (always Free!)
Seeking Fortune
Seeking Charity
Seeking Rachel
The Seeking Series
Oh Danny Boy
I Love You More
A Snowy White Christmas
A Portuguese Christmas
Holiday Hearts Book Bundle Volume One
Holiday Hearts Book Bundle Volume Two
Holiday Hearts Book Bundle Volume Three
Holiday Hearts Book Bundle Volume Four
Holiday Hearts Book Bundle Volume Five
Candleglow and Mistletoe
Maeve (Perfect Match)
A Love Song To Cherish
A Christmas To Cherish
A Valentine To Cherish

A Christmas Puppy To Cherish
A Homecoming To Cherish
A Summer To Cherish
Romance Stories To Cherish
Romance Stories To Cherish Volume Two
Cherished Hearts Six Book Volume
Aloha To Love
Sweet Peppermint Kisses
Valentine Hearts Boxed Set
1-800-CUPID
1-800-CHRISTMAS
1-800-IRELAND
1-800-SUMMER
1-800-NEW YEAR
The 1-800-Series Sweet Contemporary Romance Bundle
Irish Hearts Sweet Romance Bundle
Holly's Gift
A Chocolate-Box Christmas
A Chocolate-Box New Years
A Chocolate-Box Valentine
A Chocolate-Box Summer Breeze
A Chocolate-Box Christmas Wish
A Chocolate-Box Irish Wedding
Chocolate-Box Hearts
Chocolate-Box Hearts Volume Two
Chocolate-Box Double Hearts
Recipes From The Heart
Leading Hearts
New Year Hearts
SENIOR HEARTS
Summer Hearts
Christmas in the Air (1-800-Book)
A Very Christian Christmas
The 1-800-Series Volume Two

The 1-800-Series Complete
Christmas Tails of the Heart
Cocoa's Christmas Love
Pawfect Christmas Hearts
Pink Coral Island
Whispers of Love in Sweetwater Springs
Whispers of Maple Memories in Sweetwater Springs
Whispers of Sweetwater Springs
A Harvest of Miracles
A Winter Promise
A Season Out of Time
Hearts and Horseshoes
1-800-CUPIDON (French Edition)
1-800-CUPDO (Spanish Edition)
1-800-AMOR (German Edition)

Most books are available in ebook, audiobook, paperback,
Large Print paperback and Hardcover.
Many are FREE on Kindle Unlimited!

A GIFT FOR YOU

To keep up on newly released ebooks, paperbacks, Large Print Paperbacks, audiobooks, as well as exclusive sales, sign up for Josie's Newsletter today.

As a thank you, I'll send you a Free PDF: The Beauty Of

Josie's Newsletter

Did you know that according to a Yale University study, people who read books live longer?